Locked

# OrangeBooks Publication

1st Floor, Rajhans Arcade, Mall Road, Kohka, Bhilai, Chhattisgarh 490020

Website: **www.orangebooks.in**

---

© **Copyright, 2024, Author**

All rights reserved. No part of this book may be reproduced, stored in a retrieval system, or transmitted, in any form by any means, electronic, mechanical, magnetic, optical, chemical, manual, photocopying, recording or otherwise, without the prior written consent of its writer.

**First Edition, 2024**
**ISBN:** 978-93-6554-331-5

**I THOUGHT NYX WOULD BE THE GOOD KID WITH A PSYCHOTIC MOM, BUT SHE WAS THE SAME**

# LOCKED

### Who dies twice?
### Well, who kills twice?

## Medha Veliganti

### OrangeBooks Publication
www.orangebooks.in

# Acknowledgement

First, I'm going to thank my parents, Swapna and Siddhartha. I am eternally grateful for the sacrifices you have made. Thank you for believing in me, and inspiring me to be my best. My grandparents, Ammama, Purshi Thatha, Shantha Avva, And Thatha, have cared for and always looked out for me. Thank you for everything!

Thank you so much to my cousins, Pinky Akka, Sweety Akka, and Moni Akka for reading and reviewing my book. Thank you, Geetha Atta, for giving me corrections and reading my book!! Thank you Mahitha Atta for printing out my book's first copy and taking the time to read it!! Thank you Pranavi Atta for recommending a publishing house!! Also, my other cousins, who grew up with me. Also thank you to my school, Chrysalis High, and some of the teachers who have genuinely cared and changed my life.

Alright, now, my friends. Ok first of all to the first three people who grew up with me, and watched me do stupid things- Mythili, Viditha and Vishrutha, You guys are the OG people, now, Piyusha, thank you for always being there for me, Dhanvi, you said I'll become a billionaire if I publish this book, I'm still not one, and the first person to read this book Neeraj, Thank you for giving me suggestions for the book!

Also, I shall acknowledge myself, Medha is proud of you

# Contents

Chapter – 1 .................................................................. 1
Chapter – 2 .................................................................. 8
Chapter – 3 ................................................................ 12
Chapter – 4 ................................................................ 17
Chapter – 5 ................................................................ 20
Chapter – 6 ................................................................ 24
Chapter – 7 ................................................................ 27
Chapter – 8 ................................................................ 31
Chapter – 9 ................................................................ 37
Chapter – 10 .............................................................. 41
Chapter – 11 .............................................................. 47
Chapter – 12 .............................................................. 50
Chapter – 13 .............................................................. 57
Chapter – 14 .............................................................. 62
Chapter – 15 .............................................................. 68
Chapter – 16 .............................................................. 72
Chapter – 17 .............................................................. 75

| | |
|---|---|
| Chapter – 18 | 80 |
| Chapter – 19 | 83 |
| Chapter – 20 | 86 |
| Chapter – 21 | 90 |
| Chapter – 22 | 94 |
| Chapter – 23 | 96 |
| Chapter – 24 | 101 |
| Chapter – 25 | 105 |
| Epilogue | 107 |

# Chapter - 1

'What do you mean you're getting a divorce?' screamed Nyx as she stormed into the lavish party hall. She cried as she slumped down to the floor. A hush fell over the room as Nyx's quivering voice filled the air, 'What do you mean you are getting a divorce, Mom? her hands trembled as she gripped on to the floor, her nails screeching on the marble.

Nyx Ada's heart pounded in her chest in the opulent party hall, her eyes wide with disbelief. Alicia swiftly turned facing her, she met her daughter's gaze and squeezed her eyes.

Alicia was rich. Much more than Ryan, her husband, or should I say, Ex-Husband. She was a businesswoman and had ten mansions all over the city. She had a "not-so-legal" business, that she never revealed.

She was celebrating her 46th birthday, at a party, when Nyx came running with divorce papers in her hand.

'Nyx, I-' Alicia started, as she struts forward, she did not let Alicia continue.

Nyx's hands clenched into fists at her sides, her whole body shaking with emotion. 'But how could you do this on your birthday, Mom?' she choked out, tears welling up in her eyes. 'How could you ruin everything like this?'

All the guests looked at Alicia. There was an awkward silence.

The room felt heavy with emotions as Nyx's sobs echoed through the walls.

Alicia shot Nyx a look. 'Mom...But...' Nyx whispered in a low voice. 'GET OUT' shouted Alicia, her hands trembling, as she pointed towards the door.

As Nyx's tears blurred her vision, she ran past the security guards stationed at the gates and out into the cool night air. The sound of her footsteps against the pavement filled the silence as she raced away from the mansion. Her dad, Ryan Edin, was sitting outside the house, sulking into his hands, his shoulders bent together. Their eyes met.

"Dad..." Nyx's voice broke as she approached him, her heart heavy with the weight of their family falling apart. "What's going on? Why didn't you tell me?"

Ryan looked up: his eyes red-rimmed with tears. 'I didn't want you to get caught in the middle of this mess, Nyx,' he replied, trying not to break into tears again.

'Dad, please, you can figure this out, right?' she tried to say, wiping the tears of her face

Ryan reached into his pocket and pulled out the car keys, his jaw clenched, he drove off into the night.

Nyx fell onto the hard pavement. 'DAD! NO!!' her knees hit the concrete, blood started seeping through her torn blue jeans.

'NYX', A loud voice filled the air, Alicia had found her. 'You embarrassed me, everyone is asking me if it is true!'

Nyx's eyes blazed with anger as she struggled to her feet, her expression defiant. 'Embarrassing you?' she spat. 'Well tell them the truth! Tell them what you did to Dad!'

'THAT'S ENOUGH' Shouted Alicia, she threw her car keys at Nyx and shot her a look at the car. 'Go home now Nyx!' Nyx ran. Not to the car. She ran towards her dad's car.

Alicia picked up the divorce papers Nyx had left and strode back to the mansion, as she wiped off a single tear that ran down her cheeks. She entered the big doors towering over her and found all the guests staring at her. She had too much to deal with. She slowly picked up a glass of wine, and raised it 'To a single life,'

Everyone raised their glass.

Nyx sprinted down the darkened highway, sweat pouring down her face, hoping she would catch up with the black Audi her dad was in, but instead, she crashed into a cycle.

'MOVE' cried Nyx, as she stood up and looked into the highway.

'You can't be running around on a highway, you know,' said a deep voice. Nyx turned, a boy around her age was dusting off his shirt. 'Well? What do you want?' asked the boy. 'Nothing, you fucking ruined it, I almost caught up with the car' she blurted out as she looked at the car as it drove off into the darkness.

'Well…sometimes things happen for a reason' he mumbled.

The boy got on his cycle and said, 'I am no kidnapper, but I can help, I am pretty fast.'

Nyx nodded as a small smile appeared on her face, she got on the cycle and held on for dear life as the boy started to peddle faster and faster.

'Are you sure I can trust you?' screamed Nyx, as she tried to look straight ahead for a car.

'Yes, you can!' said the boy. 'Name?' 'Nyx', she said. 'Yours?'

'Dexter, you can call me Dex.'

As Nyx clung onto Dex's speeding bicycle, the world blurred around her as they weaved through the highway. Her heart raced. With each passing moment, the distant silhouette of the black Audi drew closer, fueling Nyx's determination to confront her father and demand answers about the sudden divorce.

The cycle zoomed past the road and came closely behind the Audi, which was driving a little slow. Suddenly the car stopped, and a man got out.

The cycle came to a screeching halt. Dexter looked up to see Nyx had broken out into a cold sweat.

Nyx gasped: it was not her dad...It was her-

'Simon?!' cried Nyx. Simon was the family butler. Not any more, he was going away with Ryan.

'Go away Nyxy' he said with a cold tone.

Nyx had never been called "Nyxy" by anyone except Simon, it was a nickname reserved just for her, a term of endearment that spoke of the special bond they shared... even though he was her bodyguard, he was like a father to her.

Nyx tapped Dex on his shoulder and whispered, 'Let's go.'

Dex nodded and he slowly turned the cycle around. They rode off into the darkness, while Nyx shed tears of anger. Simon had never been this rude or cold. Nyx was sadder about that, than the divorce.

Dex stopped after a while, he was panting heavily. 'I'm so sorry Nyx' he said.

'Can we go back, please? I just want to go back' she replied Dexter nodded and took a U-turn.

'We're here' said Nyx, as she stood in front of a huge mansion. 'Woah, you live here?' Dex asked, kicking the stand of his cycle.

'Yes. Do you want me to ask my driver to drop you home, you look tired?'

Dex, who was still looking at the huge house nodded yes, and followed Nyx inside.

Nyx smiled and sent a text to her driver, but her eyes widened as she got a text from a number she did not recognize.

TO-nyxtheada@mail.com FROM-r4455@mail.com

Stay away from her, she will kill you.

Nyx gasped loudly, her hands tightened around her phone, as her fingertips turned white, Dex came up to her.

'What happened? -' Dex stopped, as he read the message.

'Who is that' he asked leaning over her shoulder.

Nyx shrugged, reading it again and again, her eyes scanning the Email.

'Maybe a prank?' she said, switching off the phone, she slid it into her pocket, and looked up at Dex. 'You should go home, it's late.'

Dex nodded, 'Add your number, I'll text you when I get home' he said, handing his phone to her.

Nyx could not sleep.

She rolled over from her bed, reached for her phone, opened the text, and read it again. It was not a prank, she knew it, she looked at the time, 2 A.M., her mother was still not back from the party She decided to ring her.

As the phone rang, Nyx got up and looked out the window, the moon was shining brightly, lighting up the woods behind her house.

'Hello, Mom?' she said, her eyes shone, when she heard her mom on the other line.

'Yes, Nyx.'

'When are you coming home, Mom?' 'I don't know Nyx.'

'But, are you coming home now?'

'I said, I do not know, Nyx.'

'But, it's really late, I'm alone, all the maids have left.'
'We have security Nyx.'

'But mom, I-'

'Bye-' The call was cut 'Bye' she sighed!

Nyx stared at her phone for a moment, as a teardrop slid through her eyelid, falling on to her lap.

# Chapter – 2

As Alicia staggered into the grand foyer of their mansion, 'I'm going out Nyx' she called.

Nyx walked down the staircase, with bloodshot eyes.

'What?' she asked her, but then she saw the divorce papers in her hand. Alicia was going to her lawyer to sign the divorce papers. Of course.

'We have to talk, Mom,' Nyx's voice quivered with a mix of anger and despair as she pleaded for some semblance of understanding or closure in this moment of upheaval.

Alicia's detached response cut through the heavy silence like a knife. 'I don't have time for this right now' she stated flatly, her gaze distant and her tone sounded final. She turned and strode out the door. She knew Nyx wanted to talk about the divorce, no way, Alica could not let her ruin this for her, she was happy, free, peaceful. No one blocking her views, thoughts, ideas.

Nyx stared at the door as it closed. She took out her phone and texted Dexter. NYX- meet me at the park, 12 o clock.

Dex-'Ok.'

Nyx cycled into the park, making a sharp turn away from a stray cat crossing the road, she noticed Dex, sitting on the bench staring down at his phone. Nyx parked her cycle and walked over.

'Hey' she said, rubbing her palms to warm them. He did not reply, he just showed his phone to her. Nyx gasped. 'What?' she said looking at him with a worried look. r4455@mail.com had messaged him a "Stay away".

'I never give my number to random people' he said, looking away from the phone. 'Creepy, sick prank?' he said deleting the message.

Was someone watching them? Stalking them? Or was it just one big joke? Nyx sighed, her thoughts eating her up.

She nodded with a weird expression. 'I wish'

They grabbed their cycles and walked down the street; Nyx was deep in thought.

Dex noticed.' It's almost lunchtime, wanna come over?'

'Yes please, beats the lunch I get from the "Private chef" who cooks snails and calls it gourmet' she replied.

They drove into the other side of town. The normal people's side, the happy side, no entitlements. Away from the high-rise apartments and the "rich" neighborhood.

'Well, we're here!' said Dex.

'My mom's name is Dian, and my dad is Dev', he said, enlightening Nyx. Nyx looked at him weirdly 'OK?' she laughed as she rolled up her sleeves.

They walked up to the front door, which was decorated with lights and a small sign read- Happy Diwali!

Dex rang the doorbell, and a short lady opened the door. 'Hi Dexi, oh! and hi-' she put her hands on the door.

'Nyx, Nyx Ada' she stammered.

Dian smiled 'Hi Nyx, come in dear!' She gestured her hand into the house.

The house was beautiful. It was bright, the sun shone through the big windows, the fireplace had flower decorations, the TV was playing "Say Yes to the Dress."

Her attention was drawn to the dining table set with an array of dishes, their vibrant colors and tantalizing aromas hinting her nose. She couldn't help but smile at the sight, it looked happy.

Dev Kumar walked in from the kitchen; his hands full of fresh laundry. 'Dev! meet Nyx! She is Dexi's new friend!' Dian said giving him a wink. Dev smiled warmly. ' Sit down, while we set the table. '

Nyx nodded and walked with Dex over to the couch. 'Dexi?' giggled Nyx 'Your mom calls you Dexi?'

Dex looked away embarrassed, smiling.

Nyx's gaze momentarily shifted away. As she soaked in the cozy embrace of Dex's family home, the contrast between the vibrant warmth surrounding her and the icy grip of her haunted past, was like a slap in the face. The sun's gentle rays caressed the room, painting everything in a soft glow, while the laughter and chatter of Dex's family filled the air.

Her green eyes watering with fresh tears.

Nyx blinked back tears, feeling overwhelmed by the contrast between the vibrant warmth of Dex's family home and the icy grip of her messed up family. Dex noticed her emotional reaction and gently asked, 'Hey, are you okay?'

She wasn't, she couldn't, everything's hurt, she felt betrayed by her mom and dad. The wounds left by her fractured relationship with her parents, felt raw and unhealed like an open wound.

'I'm OK.'

# Chapter – 3

"Ugh, come on, Nyx! It's just one party," Alicia exclaimed impatiently. Nyx slumped down; her frustration evident. "Mom, I hate parties," she groaned, flinging her shoes aside without a care, the Nikes rolled down and fell. Alicia waved off Nyx's protests. "Take your friend, Rex, right?" she quipped, not bothering to get the name right, why would she? She was Alicia Ada, the most powerful woman in the city. Nyx rolled her eyes dramatically. "It's Dexter, Mom. I really don't wanna go, but whatever," she muttered, resigned to her fate, she sighed as she pulled her black hair into a ponytail, as a few strands fell on her face, she squinted her eyes, "Do I have to go-". With a dismissive gesture, Alicia declared, "You're going, end of story.

Now go get dressed, the drivers dropping you."

'It's not like you're not going to stay there anyway, why do you want me to go?'

'You're my daughter, you have to.'

Nyx 'Hey, mom wants us to go to some party, are you coming?' 'Dex- Ok'? ''ll be there, as long as there's cake'-

Nyx, 'It's not that kind of party Dex'…

Nyx threw on a jacket as she sauntered out of her room, spotting Dexter maneuvering his bike into the driveway, his cycle shone in the setting-sun. As the doorman swung the door open, her mom's voice called out, "Hi, Rex?" filled the air. Dexter corrected her with a smirk, "It's Dex, but sure, Rex works just fine too." he said brushing his fingers through his hair.

"Let's go," Nyx declared nonchalantly, making her way down the stairs, she held on the rail for grip, as she stumbled in her heels.

Dexter glanced up "Hey" Nyx responded with a wry smile, "Let's get this party over with."

Meanwhile, Alicia grabbed her Birkin bag and strutted outside, her heels echoing on the floor.

"Man, your mom is something else," Dexter remarked. Nyx gave him an amused once-over and quipped, "She's a LOT" Dexter chuckled, trying not to sound stupid; after all, he couldn't afford to mess up in front of a millionaire.

As they stepped outside, Nyx was taken aback by what awaited them. "A limo? Seriously, Mom?" she protested, a hint of exasperation in her voice.

Alicia's tone turned cold, her eyes piercing into Nyx's "I have somewhere to be later. So just get in."

Dexter looked impressed, as he got in, he touched the leather seats and admired the interior of the Limo. Nyx just sat, looking bored, she was sick of it, she was sick of being rich, and having too much of anything sucked. She switched her phone on, when it glowed from a notification.

She had a friend request from a person called r4455iley on snapchat. Nyx read the name without the numbers, Riley, she did not know anyone called Riley.

'What the-, check this out' she said, pulling Dexter's jacket so he would pay attention.

'What' gasped Dex as he read the name. Nyx noticed his eyes widened. Dex looked up at her.

Alicia noticed the kids. 'What is it' she said looking up from her phone. Nyx looked at Dex, 'Nothing'.

Nyx leaned back into the leather seats, sighing. Who was Riley? She heard it somewhere, but where? Riley. R I L E Y. Where had she heard it?

After a short drive, they were in front of Dollar View Mansion 204. Colette's house. Alicia stepped out. 'Mom, where are you going?' asked Nyx as she got down with Dex. 'I just want to say hello to Coco' said Alicia. 'Coco?' asked Nyx.

'Collete.'

Nyx nodded sarcastically, of course, her mom had a nickname for her friends. Everyone except her. It was just Nyx. Nyxy. Only Simon calls her that.

Nyx knocked on the door. Loud party music and people screaming and singing came pouring out as Collete opened the door. 'Mrs. Ada!, Hello! ' She said.

Collete, ignoring Nyx and Dexter. Straight up? IGNORE? LIKE NYX AND DEX WEREN'T HUMANS? AT LEAST SHE COULD HAVE LOOKED AT THEM

RIGHT? Calm down Nyx thought, her mind cursing Collete, or should I say "Coco."

'Hi Coco, sweetie, how are you?' 'I'm fine Mrs. Ada, come in, please.'

'It's Ms. Ada now dear! Anyways I have to go, just wanted to pop in and say hi to my Coco!' she laughed.

Collete smiled and gave her a very "posh" hug, they bid goodbye, and Collete looked at Nyx and Dex was disgusted 'Are you gonna stand there or come in?' she asked in a different tone. Dex smiled awkwardly and walked in with Nyx. 'No need to be an Ass-' Nyx mumbled, but Collete had already run off. Nyx walked in, looking around, oh god. This was going to be a hard day, she noticed much of her class was there.

The house party was a chaotic scene of debauchery. Lisa Rain, a so-called "prostitute" stood next to the speakers as she swayed to the loud music, beer spilling from her cup. David Weir and Risha were making out, and Felix was eating a chicken wing. Teenagers stumbling around in a drunken haze. Layla Sian was there too, her blue hair covering forehead. The music blared at ear-splitting levels, and Nyx closed her eyes. She hated it. Maria Singh was screaming into her phone, the girl always had issues with her parents, just like Nyx. The air was thick with the scent of alcohol and sweat, as bodies pressed together in the living room that was now a dance floor. Max Ohm was on the floor, picking his wallet, and the kitchen was a mess of spilled drinks and discarded red cups. Nyx looked at each and every one of them in disgust.

Dex took one look at Nyx and took her to an empty corner where a girl had passed out, Daisy Lynn. 'Let's get out of here Dexter' Nyx whispered.

Outside, groups of teenagers gathered on the lawn, shouting and laughing as they smoked and drank under the dim glow of the streetlights. The noise from the party could be heard echoing down the street, drawing angry glances from neighbors.

Nyx looked in a secluded corner of the yard, a group of teens huddled together, their faces contorted in concentration as they each took turns sniffing a white powdery substance from a small baggy. The air was thick with tension and the unmistakable scent of drugs. Nyx looked away. Why did she recognize that smell? She never did drugs, did her maids use it? Bodyguards? Driver? Or Simon? No way. What's wrong with you, Nyx thought to herself.

Dex grabbed a paper airplane that was left on the ground and threw it up in the air, it flew up across the dark clouds coming near them. A huge thunder roared, scaring everyone. Nyx ran her hand through her hair, as it flew in the wind, her hands covered her face as she felt a drop of water hit her eye, and another.

# Chapter – 4

TO-nyxtheada@mail.com FROM-r4455@mail.com

There is a lot you do not know. Please stay safe.

Nyx's hands trembled with anger as she flung her phone across the bed, the device bouncing off the soft mattress before skidding to a stop on the floor. 'Oh god,' she mumbled. What did Nyx not know? Who was this r4455, or "Riley"? Nyx grabbed her phone that was on the floor and scanned through her contacts to see if there was anyone named Riley.

No luck. R I L E Y. Who was it?

Nyx covered her eyes with her hands. Deep in thought. Think Nyx, think she thought. She heard her mom screaming at someone, Nyx thought it would be a house staff, as usual, but she went out of her room anyway, she was thirsty, and a glass of water sounded enjoyable, she hadn't stepped out her room anyway since the morning. Nyx stopped; Alicia was shouting at-Simon.

Simon stood there looking Alicia dead in the eye, his hands in his pockets, as she called the security. He noticed Nyx looking down at him from the staircase.

'Hello Nyxy' he said calmly.

Nyx did not reply. She looked at her mom, who was tensed and worried. Alicia was never like that. She never cared about anything other than herself and her money. She may appear classy on the outside but has a lot of secrets inside.

Simon looked at Alicia again, 'You have done the wrong thing Ms. Ada. Let him be......'

Alicia was pissed, her forehead tensed up, as beads of sweat wet down her hair.

Simon walked off, leaving a trail of confusion.

Nyx went back to her room; she wondered what was that wrong thing Simon was talking about. Was it about divorcing her husband, Ryan Edin? Or something related to the business?

Nyx sat in her room, staring out the window as the rain poured down outside. The sound of thunder rumbled in the distance, adding to the eerie atmosphere. Suddenly, a strange figure appeared at the window on the third floor, causing Nyx to let out an ear-piercing scream.

As the figure came closer, Nyx realized it was Dex. She let out a sigh of relief and laughed at his clumsy attempts to climb through the window. Dex finally managed to get inside, dripping wet from the rain.

'What are you doing here?' Nyx asked, still chuckling.

Shaking off the rain from his hair, he said 'I thought I'd come over and see if you wanted to hang out.' Nyx got up and reached for a towel on her chair, she tossed it over to him. They started talking.

The rain continued to drum against the window, a soothing backdrop to their conversation. Nyx and Dex laughed, shared secrets, and talked about bitchy friends. They had a lot in common. As the night wore on, they eventually fell into a comfortable silence, the only sound the soft patter of raindrops against the window.

As it grew late, Dex realized that he had to leave before the storm worsened. Nyx walked him to the window, he came from. Dex flashed her a mischievous grin before attempting to climb out the window once again.' Ouch, this was easier when I got in.'

Nyx couldn't help but laugh, again, her laughter mixing with the sound of rain outside. Dex paused for a moment, his hand resting on the windowsill as he looked back at Nyx with a warm smile. 'Well bye then' he said his hands gripping on as he held on.

Nyx nodded. 'Don't get caught in the rain again Dexi.' 'Shut up.'

Dex left, leaving Nyx alone in her room. The room felt emptier without him, the silence more pronounced. As she settled back into her bed, Nyx closed her eyes. But she couldn't help but think, who was

R I L E Y?

# Chapter - 5

Nyx stood in the middle of her garden, looking around for some flowers to send over to Dex's house, because Diwali was coming soon. As she strolled around, she noticed a black van that had stopped in front of her mansion. Its tinted windows conceal the occupants inside. The vehicle looks worn and battered, with scratches and dents marring its exterior. Alicia emerges from the mansion, her designer clothes and expensive jewelry contrasting with the shadiness of the van. She approaches the vehicle with a briefcase in hand. The lady hands over the briefcase to a guy.

The van speeds off into the night, leaving behind a cloud of suspicion and intrigue. 'Mom, who was that?' asked Nyx. Alicia turned around in surprise.

'Nyx! Oh god, you scared me!' she replied, dusting off her hands, with a sigh of relief.

'Who was that?' Nyx asked again.

'No one Nyx, work-related' Alicia snarled not making eye contact with her 'Sure Mom' said Nyx sarcastically.

She walked off leaving her mom standing alone on the grand pathway into the house.

Nyx grabbed a small bag in the kitchen, loading it with some flowers and a small box of cookies, she grabbed her cycle keys and walked back out to grab her cycle. She drove it out and saw Alicia furiously texting on her phone, she looked tensed. Nyx rolled her eyes and looked away.

She drove while listening to "Gimme More" by Britney Spears. Her Dad's favorite singer. He used to come down the stairs in the morning singing "HIT ME, BABY, ONE MORE TIME". Nyx smiled thinking about those times. They were happy.

She parked her bike in the driveway of Dexter's house and walked up to the door, Dian was outside decorating the windows, she smiled at Nyx.

'Hello, Nyx!'

Nyx waved, 'Hello Mrs. Dev! I brought over some flowers for decoration!'

'Thank you, dear! Dexi is in his room!' Replied Dian as she got down a tiny ladder while hanging up lights.

Nyx pushed open the door and left the bag on a small table. She walked upstairs over to Dex's room. 'Dex? You there?' she called out. Dex jumped up from his bed. 'NYX' he screamed. 'What?' asked Nyx looking at his worried face.

Dex jumped off his bed grabbed his laptop and shoved it to her face TO- dev_dex08@mail.com

FROM-r4455@mail.com Hi Dexter. Be careful.

Nyx gasped. 'What is this?' Her mind racing, as she held onto the laptop.

Dex scratched his head 'I don't know...am I going to die' he said with a nervous chuckle.

'Not funny Dexter' Nyx said, still looking worried. Dex closed his laptop. He put it away. 'Trust me, it's a sick prank.'

Nyx looked up at him 'Ok, ok.'

Dex smiled, as he grabbed his phone and got up, 'let's go down.'

They went down and saw Dian sitting on the couch eating the cookies Nyx had brought over. 'Honey, these are amazing!' she said as she stuffed her mouth. 'Our chef made them' replied Nyx smiling.

Her phone rang, it was Alicia. 'Nyx, come home.'

'Mom, I just got to my friend's house...'

'You can go back later Nyx, you come home now' 'Why?'

'I need to go somewhere, you need to stay home' 'Mom, can't I?'

'Now, Nyx.'

Nyx hung up and looked over at Dex, who heard the whole conversation. 'Well, I got to go' she said. Dex nodded sadly. 'Bye, call me if you need anything.'

Nyx nodded and said bye to Dian, who was thoroughly enjoying the cookies. She rode back to her house, and as she approached the driveway, she saw her mom. Alicia elegantly strolled into her mansion's driveway; her designer heels clicked against the pavement. That sound drove Nyx crazy. The gleaming Rolls-Royce awaited her, a symbol of her success and luxury. Alicia looked out and waved Nyx a bye.

Nyx got off her cycle and pushed it into the driveway, as two maids came running behind her, asking if they could help her. She ignored them as she walked inside and noticed a phone on the table next to the door. 'Whose is this?' she asked a maid.

'It is Simons, Miss. He dropped it in the garden when he came to visit' Nyx nodded as she picked it up and took it upstairs.

# Chapter – 6

She tossed around in bed, trying to open Simons 's phone, it had a passcode that was letters. Nyx wondered if she could find any clues on why her dad left so abruptly, maybe a text message on his phone would explain it? Why was Simon threatening Alicia with some "messages" he would tell someone?

After several failed attempts to break into the phone, she let out a frustrated sigh. What if his password was after his kid's name? She knew he had a daughter, but Nyx could not remember the name, so she decided to text her mom asking about it.

NYX- 'Hey, random question, Simon had a kid, right?'

MOM- 'Yes, why, do you have to remind me of him, I was having a good day' NYX- 'OK. Just asking...what was her name again?'

MOM- 'Whose?' NYX- 'Simon's kid.' MOM- 'Riley.'

It can't be. No. Nyx did not know Riley that much. And besides, why would Riley do that to her anyway? Right?

Nyx typed in the name. Bingo. The phone was unlocked, Nyx scanned through the text messages but had no luck. She was reading the conversation between her dad and Simon, but nothing weird. She tried searching for her mom's conversation, but it was not there. Maybe Simon had deleted it? Nyx sighed. She opened mail. And noticed Simon had two accounts, simon1975@mail.com and r4455@mail.com.

What the actual fuck.

Nyx looked at her screen wide-eyed. It was no doubt, Simons's daughter Riley was sending those messages. But why? Riley never really met up with Nyx.

She would visit sometimes, during big parties and events. They talked for a few minutes, that's all. Nyx never really told her a lot of stuff. They just knew each other. But Nyx knew Riley was a bitch. The way Riley used to talk, with that attitude, it bugged her. She was a pretty girl, with pretty hair, and had the "perfect body". That was all Nyx knew about Riley.

The bell rang. Nyx never really went down to open the door, the maids did it. But she peeked out of her room down the huge hallway, and through the big glass window next to the door was Simon. Nyx rushed down. She knew he was there for the phone, and she opened the big door.

Simon smiled. It was warm and felt homely. Something Nyx hadn't felt in a while, her eyes glinting, as she shook her hair off her face.

'You left your phone here' she said handing the phone over to Simon. 'Thank you Nyxy' said Simon taking the phone from her hands.

'I was wondering... how's Riley?' she asked leaning on the door 'She great' said Simon, he was surprised she knew her name.

'Is it ok if I come by sometime and say hello...she's nice, a good friend' asked Nyx.

'Sure, maybe next week?'

Nyx nodded, saying goodbye. She watched Simon walk off into his car. He looked a little tensed.

She would soon find out what these messages meant.

She had to tell Dexter about it. He was getting messages from r4455 too. Wait, what if Riley wanted to kill them? But why the fuck would she?

Confusing shit, eh? Nyx wondered.

She immediately texted him and asked him to come over.
NYX- Come over. now.

# Chapter – 7

'Wait so you think a random girl "Riley" who is your Ex-butler's daughter is sending us messages...and you don't know anything about her, and you think she's a weirdo?' Dex asked as he walked beside Nyx. She nodded, 'I'm meeting her next week'. Dex stopped, 'Oh god Nyx. The things you do' he said looking her up and down.

She looked annoyed, as she slicked her hair back. They walked inside, stepping into Nyx's house, she turned around quickly. She felt like someone or something was watching them, she looked around. Nothing, she couldn't shake the feeling of unease.

She scanned the shadows, searching for any sign of movement or presence. The hair on the back of her neck stood on end as she strained her senses, she held her knees as they got weak, the atmosphere crackled with tension as Nyx scanned the surroundings. She did not know why. Dex looked back. 'What?' he asked, as he put his phone down on the glass table. 'I think someone is in here' she whispered.

'You live in a huge ass mansion, with like twenty-five security guards and forty maids and chefs, of course there are people in here Nyx, I don't know why you would be-' he stopped, 'fuck- fuck- Nyx, Look behind you- Fuck-'

Something moved behind a tree in her big garden. Nyx's heart raced, and she looked over at Dex, he saw it. 'Nah... I saw it' said Dex.

'SECURITY' screamed Nyx, a guy came running. 'Yes miss?' he asked. 'Can you check if there is something behind that tree?' she said pointing at a tall, bushy tree. The security jogged over and looked around. 'NOTHING MISS' he shouted. Nyx nodded and walked inside with Dex. He looked back worriedly and watched Nyx shut the door.

'So, what's the plan?' he asked.

'Well, I'm meeting her next week, right, so Imma get some dirt on her, be extra nice to her and you know act like she's my BFF' said Nyx sarcastically.

'But you don't know anything about her'

Nyx smirked 'Well, good thing I'm a skilled predator when it comes to stalking.' Dex looked at her and burst out laughing, as he held his stomach in pain 'Shut the fuck up-' Nyx said looking at Dex.

She took out her laptop and googled Riley Simon.

There was an Instagram ID- rileyyyysimxn_stxr, Nyx clicked on it. It was public. Nyx sighed a sigh of happiness. 'Here goes nothing', she said as she went through all the pictures, there were around thirty posts. She scanned through the pictures, Dex leaned over and said 'Damn...that's Riley?' Nyx nodded, noticing the glint in his eyes. 'It looks like she likes singing' said Nyx, looking at all the pictures Riley posted when she was singing on stage, and all the awards she had won. Nyx looked away annoyed. 'Well, I'll figure something out.'

'You know how to sing, if you do, maybe you guys can get closer, you know-?' asked Dexter.

'I sound like a dying cat,' she replied, pushing him off her chair.

Nyx had been mindlessly scrolling through Riley's Instagram feed, feeling a mix of envy and curiosity as she looked at her perfectly curated life. She finally tore her eyes away from the screen and set her phone aside. 'This bitch looks so annoying; I just want to punch her.'

'For fucks sake, calm down, you don't even know her'
'Fuck off.'

As she turned to look out the large window, she noticed the darkness outside and the faint glow of streetlights in the distance. Suddenly, her attention was drawn to a figure moving in the shadows. It was too far away to make out any details, but Nyx felt a shiver run down her spine as she watched the mysterious figure. Dex gasped. 'No way, it's back.'

As Nyx and Dex approached the window, their hearts raced with anticipation. The figure outside was moving closer. Nyx felt fear and curiosity as she squinted to get a better look. The person was dressed in all black, their face obscured by a hood. They moved with an eerie grace, almost gliding along the pavement. She pressed her face against the cold glass, trying to catch a glimpse of the person's features. It looked like-

'Wait, where did it go?' asked Dex looking around, fucking up Nyx's thoughts 'DEXTER, I almost recognised it- Fuck' she said her hands sweaty, as they pressed against the glass window.

# Chapter - 8

Nyx stared at her reflection in the mirror, her heart racing. It was the day. She was going to meet Riley, why did this sound so easy when she thought about it? She stood in front of her mirror fixing her hair, brushing out the same black curl of hair. She felt a mix of emotions swirling inside of her, she looked down at her phone, which lit up as a new message from r4455 popped up. Nyx didn't bother opening it, she was meeting with r4455, right?

Right?

Right. She was, who else was r4455? It was Riley, it was obvious.

Alicia walked in, looking at her. 'Why the fuck do you want to meet Riley.' she asked, looking disgusted. Nyx looked away from the mirror and turned to her mom. 'Just wanted to reunite with an old friend.'

'Old friend, Nyx, you know damn well that Riley was never your friend' laughed Alicia looking at Nyx narrow-eyed. 'What?' asked Nyx, clenching her fists,' We were friends, you know, not like you know anything about my life.'

Nyx sighed, knowing her mother was right, she took a deep breath 'I need to face her, Mom. I need to confront her about something.' Alicia nodded, unbothered. 'Well, come down fast, the car's waiting'. She walked off, leaving Nyx alone.

The Lamborghini rolled into the driveway with a throaty roar, its sleek and aerodynamic design catching the sunlight and gleaming in the midday sun. Nyx stood outside her mansion. The sound of the engine reverberated through the air, sending a shiver down Nyx's spine, she was terrified of asking Riley about the "messages".

Nyx got into the Lamborghini, the luxurious leather seats enveloping her in comfort as she settled in. She took out her phone, her fingers tapping on the screen. She was letting Dex know she was going. The driver glanced at her through the rearview mirror.

'Where to, Miss?' he inquired, his voice smooth and professional. 'Simon's house,' Nyx replied, her tone firm. The driver's eyebrows shot up in surprise. 'The old butler's house?' he asked, not sounding so professional anymore, a hint of disbelief in his voice. Nyx simply nodded; her jaw set with determination. Even though her heart was beating out her chest.

As the Lamborghini glided through the streets, the driver stole occasional glances at Nyx in the rearview mirror, curiosity, and intrigue evident in his eyes. Nyx sat in silence looking out the window. The car eventually came to a stop in front of an Apartment, Misty Brooke Apartments.

'Should I do this?' Nyx sighed, she had to, and why was Riley even sending her those……

Focus Nyx, Focus, she thought, trying to push away all the questions.

She stepped out, clutching her Chanel bag, slammed the door shut, and walked up to the front, Simon's house was on the ground floor. She took a deep breath and knocked on the door. 'Oh god' she held the wall, and leaned on it, trying to calm her nerves. Why was she so nervous? She was just meeting some random girl, it's not like she would kill her, or slip something into her drink. NYX FOCUS, the voice in her head screamed, 'right' she responded to her voice, oh shit, she heard footsteps, Nyx turned away facing the exit, she should prepare to run right? What if- The door slowly creaked open.

As the door slowly creaked open, Nyx's breath caught in her chest at the sight of Riley standing before her. There she was, the perfect girl, her hair cascading down her shoulders. 'Yes?' she asked. Riley's voice was beautiful and perfect. Of course. She was a singer. 'Umm, can I help you?' she asked again, stepping outside. Weird, Nyx thought Riley would be scared, and terrified that Nyx found out who r4455 was. But no, Riley stood, eyeing the Chanel bag. Nyx pushed it behind her trying to get Riley's focus back on her.

She shivered; this was the girl who was sending those weird messages. RIGHT? Oh god Nyx, answer her, before she slams the door in your face she thought 'I'm Nyx. Nyx Ada, your dad is our butler' replied Nyx.

'Was your butler' she snarled, eyeing the Chanel bag Nyx was trying to hide. 'Right...well, I wanted to catch up with you!' Nyx said smiling awkwardly.

'Catch up about what Nyx Ada' Riley leaned on the door frame, crossing her hands, her fingernails digging into her pale skin.

'Umm...' Nyx scratched her neck looking over at the side, trying to think of something. Nyx come on, think, what and WHY would you want to catch up with Riley? She thought, looking over at her.

Simon walked up to Riley, he looked over at Nyx. 'Hello, Nyx. Riley, please take her to your room'. He said, trying to break the tension between the girls.

Nyx looked at Simon weirdly. Riley smiled sarcastically at her and started showing her to her room. The house was dirty, the living room had a small balcony that had lights hung up. There was barely any light in the main bedroom. Riley's mom, Patricia looked like she hadn't bathed in a while, she had scars all over her face, and marks on her hands. Nyx looked at the marks wide eyed, could it be- Heroin? Was she injecting it? No, Nyx was overthinking, she was nervous. 'Who's she?' asked Patricia, chewing on a bag of chips.

'Nyx Ada.' said Riley trying not to sound annoyed.

'Ada? Oh. Hi' she replied as she turned on the TV, while glancing at her husband. It was obvious, she was wondering why she had come here, to their tiny little house away from the mansion.

Nyx smiled awkwardly, as she followed Riley into her room. It was lifeless, the window was closed, and the bed was messy. The wall was covered with pictures of Riley singing, and awards she won. Riley sat on her bed and took out her phone and scrolled through her Instagram feed.

Nyx sat awkwardly on the edge. She looked around the tiny room. Even though they were kind of poor, Riley was definitely a spoiled rat. Yes, a rat, not a brat. She looked over at Riley. 'So... Riley, what do you like to do...sing?' Riley looked up 'Yes.'

She put her phone aside and turned to her 'Look, I know your mom forced you to come here and have a pity party with me, you can do whatever, you don't have to force talk with me'. Nyx looked surprised, 'No... I wanted to meet up...'

'Mhm, meet up?'

'Hey...Umm...Is this your snap?' asked Nyx leaning over with her phone showing the r4455iley ID.

Riley stared at the ID for a couple of seconds. Nyx's heart raced. It had to be, it had to. Please, please, please.

'No.'

'What?' Nyx looked away from the phone. 'But...'

'It's not mine, why would I send you a request?' she hissed Nyx sighed and texted Dexter.

NYX- I asked her. She said it's not her ID DEX- Well get more info, good luck.

NYX- I better get back, bye. DEX- Bye, FOCUS NYX.

# Chapter – 9

Nyx got up from the bed, she had enough.

'Well, explain this!' she said, shoving the messages from r445@mail Nyx confronted Riley about the messages. Gosh, finally.

Riley looked surprised; her eyes widened when she saw the mail ID.

'That's my mail...but I never sent you those texts!' she said, staring at the bright screen, her eyes squinting.

Nyx rolled her eyes 'Yeah right...look if you are jealous of me, just admit it, you do not have to be so stuck up about it. And how do you know Dexter?'

'Me? Jealous? About what? And who the fuck is Dexter?'

'My house, my money, I'm rich, you are not' she said wiping her sweaty palms on the bed.

'You might be rich, but you're a fucking bitch about it.'
'Me, a bitch? Look who's talking.'

Nyx got up, grabbed her bag, and started to walk out of the room.

Riley got up, 'Look, I'm sorry for being rude, but I actually did not send those texts...'

Nyx turned around 'Then someone magically got into your mail and hacked it and decided to text me and my friend out of all people?!' she said sarcastically.

Riley shrugged 'Maybe?'

Nyx sighed. 'Why would anyone send those to me?' she buried her face in her hands and leaned onto the wall, she was confused and she hated that look on Riley's face.

Nyx's phone got a message. TO-nyxtheada@mail.com FROM-r4455@mail.com

I see you are figuring it out. Nyx. Please.

Her eyes widened in shock, she looked over at Riley, who looked at the confused expression on Nyx's face. Nyx turned her phone towards Riley. She gasped. Her phone was on the bed, it was not Riley sending it.

'I'm sorry' Nyx said, as she slipped her phone into her bag. 'Yeah, well, whatever.' Riley whispered.

'Did you share your ID with anyone?'

Riley nodded no, she looked away and wiped a tear off her face. 'Hey, what's wrong?' Nyx said coming closer.

'My dad lost his only job, because of you stupid Mom, we lost all our money... He had savings, but they just vanished' she said crying.

Nyx felt like an asshole, she should have known Riley was going through a lot. Her mom fired her dad.

'Either my dad is spending it on something illegal like I don't know, Drugs or gambling, which I'm sure he won't, or someone fucking stole it from him. He won't tell' she cried.

Nyx put her hand through Riley's and tapped her on the shoulder.

She could see the pain and frustration in Riley's eyes, and it broke her heart.

'I'm so sorry.' Nyx said softly, squeezing Riley's hand in comfort. Riley nodded trying to hide her face. They sat in silence for a moment.

Riley wiped her tears and pulled her hand away from Nyx's grasp. She looked at her with a hint of resentment in her eyes.

'You don't understand, Nyx. You don't know what it's like to struggle like this, it's tough, you're safe in your little mansion.' Riley said, her voice tinged with bitterness. Nyx felt a pang of hurt at Riley's words.

'I'm here Riley, I can help,' Nyx said, trying to comfort her. Riley scoffed and turned away. Riley couldn't shake the feeling of resentment towards her. Nyx lived in a luxurious house, wore designer clothes, and never seemed to worry about money, she had it all, every fucking thing. It only served to remind Riley of the struggles she and her family were facing. Riley took a deep breath 'I was jealous of you, your perfect life.'

Nyx laughed awkwardly, 'You're jealous? ' 'I've been a bitch to you. I'm sorry.'

Nyx nodded and hugged her.' A good bitch.'

Who thought that Nyx Ada would even touch Riley? The daughter of a big-shot so-called "Mafia" CEO, Alicia Ada's daughter, hugs the butler's kid. Damn.

But who was r4455?

# Chapter – 10

Nyx walked out of the building. She just made friends with"r4455" who was not that bad, I guess. She sighed as she took out her phone, Dex was gonna hate her.

'Hello'

'Hey Nyx, did you get dirt on Riley?'

'Look. You should come home, or wait, come to the park near Dollar View, I need to tell you something.'

'Alright, see you there, Bye.' 'Yeah, Bye.'

Nyx put her phone away and made her way to the park. The sun was shining brightly in the clear blue sky, casting a warm glow over the busy streets, she turned right, facing the park entrance, and she walked in slowly... The sound of chirping birds and rustling leaves filled the air, a contrast to the noisy streets she had just left behind. She walked around waiting for Dexter to show up.

Nyx wandered along the winding paths. She found a quiet spot near a pond and sat down on a bench, closing her eyes and breathing in the fresh, clean air. Something her house did not have.

If Riley wasn't r4455, then who was? Or was Riley lying? Nyx leaned on the bench trying to think straight.

She heard a familiar voice calling her name. Turning around, she saw Dexter walking towards her with a serious expression on his face, Nyx twitched, he never looked like that. 'Nyx, can we talk for a minute?' Dexter asked, stopping right in front of her, his tone indicating that he had something important on his mind.

'Hey, Dex, I thought I was the one with something important to tell...but hey, go on' Nyx said.

Dex sat next to her and let out a loud sigh, 'I was cycling over, and when I went past your house, I heard your mom screaming into her phone, and I stopped my cycle and had to listen, I know, I know, bad idea, anyways, she suddenly stopped shouting and then I took out my phone and recorded this, don't get mad at me but I thought it might be about the divorce or something' he said, as he played a recording on his phone.-

"Fine I'll get the twenty bags of it later, now just get me that money, also if he says another WORD, take him to the warehouse, I'll meet you there, we will make sure that man does not see daylight again" she coughed and the recording stopped.

As the words played out, Nyx's eyes widened in shock and disbelief. 'What the actual fuck.'

Dexter looked at Nyx, his eyes reflecting the gravity of the situation. 'I don't know what's going on, Nyx, but I thought you should know. Your mom might be involved in something really serious,' he said, his voice filled with concern, as he kicked a stone away from him.

As Nyx tried to make sense of the shocking revelation, she realized that she was now faced with a dilemma that could change everything she thought, she knew about her family. Her mom was a drug dealer? A murderer? Both? What was she? Her mind was spinning.

She had to find out. Despite the urge to confront her mother further, Nyx found herself hesitating, unsure of how to proceed. The truth she had uncovered was overwhelming, and she needed time to process it all. How could she?

'Where is the "Warehouse?" Is it like behind your mansion or something?' asked Dex interrupting her thoughts.

'Much, much worse than that' Nyx whispered picking up her bag,

'It's abandoned in the woods behind our house, at least that's the one I think it is.'

'Woah.'

'We need to find out what is going on Dex!' 'Right, so what do we do?'

'Go to the warehouse, obvi' said Nyx looking him up and down 'Yes Mam. Let's go.'

They walked over to Nyx's house, where they spotted Alicia getting into her car.

'Hey, Mom, where are you going?' asked Nyx as she walked over 'Friends house, Bye' she said rolling up the window.

Nyx smirked as she saw the car speed off towards the woods. Perfect 'Let's go' she said grabbing her cycle.

As they navigated through the dense forest, Nyx and Dex relied on their keen sense of direction and the dim light filtering through the trees to guide them. They were in the woods. The sound of their cycles crunching on the forest floor echoed through the silent woods. Spooky right? Nope. Nyx was more worried about her mom.

'Oh my god, this is creepy' huffed Dex, as he stopped his cycle to look around 'I know, never been in here' Nyx said, looking back at him.

'Wait, so you don't know where the creepy ass warehouse is, you know this is the place the "Slasher", the serial killer dude, who killed like five people and left their skin hanging on trees?'

'Nope, but I'll figure it out, worst case, we get lost, and our skin will be hanging on trees too.'

'Nyx, come on' pleaded Dex looking around, pulling his jacket tighter.

After what feels like hours of searching, they finally stumble upon the abandoned warehouse, they were looking for. The building looms ominously in front of them, its windows shattered and its walls covered in graffiti. Nyx and Dex park their cycles outside and cautiously approach the entrance, their hearts pounding with excitement and fear.

'Wow, ghosts are real...What if this is where the "Slasher" kept all his bodies?'

Dex asked.

'Maybe, what if they are still there?' she eyed him, with a glint in her eyes 'Oh shut up.'

'Shit, I hear cars, go under that bush' said Nyx pushing him down.

They stayed for a while, as they watched two men walk out and one opened the door.

Alicia stepped out; she walked in holding a gun.

'Yo, I think your mom is going to kill someone,' whispered Dex.

'No way, I don't know...' Of course she was going to kill. She will. Nyx knew it. The look in Alicia's eyes.

Another black car came. This time two women came out from the front and opened the door. A tall man covered with a hood was pushed out. His head was covered and his hands were tied.

'Yup. Someone is dying', Dexter sighed.

Loud voices could be heard in the warehouse, Nyx heard her mom scream 'You dog, I'm killing you today, YOU BETRAYED ME, THE BUSINESS, YOU WANTED TO SET US UP?'

Nyx gulped. Her forehead wet, she wiped it off, trying to focus on the voices. 'Go to HELL ' Alicia shouted.

The deafening crack split the silence like a thunderclap, sending a shockwave of fear through the air. The echo of the gunshot reverberated through the warehouse. Nyx gasped, and held on to the ground, her palm sticky from sweat. The shirt stuck to her hand, as she gripped her hands, her fingernails digging into the ground.

Dex gasped, 'What the fuck, your mom really killed someone.'

Nyx stayed silent, her hands digging deeper into the ground, as the dirt went into her fingernails. She watched as they took the man whose head was hanging back into the car, the black bag covering his face and his pants stained, there was blood pouring from his arm. Alicia as usual, unfazed, walked out and stepped into her car, as her guards opened the door, they drove off.

'Let's go in' Nyx hissed, cursing her mom in her mind, why the fuck did she do that, whom did she kill? Why did she kill?

'I'll stay here, you know, keep a look out' Dex said, trying to sound brave, even though he was shivering, not from the cold.

'Alright' she whispered, wiping her sticky palms to her jeans, as she shook the leaves of her head. She could hear the gun sound still echoing, it never left her.

She held her breath.

# Chapter – 11

Nyx cautiously stepped into the dimly lit warehouse, the sound of the gunshot echoing in the empty space, it wasn't the gun, it was her footsteps, 'Focus, Nyx', she said to herself trying to block the sound. The musty smell of old wood and dust filled her nostrils as she scanned the room, her eyes adjusting to the darkness. She wiped off beads of sweat from her neck, why was she sweating? It was cold. Her knees trembling, as she tried to stay focused. The dirt from her hands slid off and fell on the wooden floor.

As she moved further into the warehouse, she noticed blood on the floor, dark red, all over, and the smell hanging in the air, she saw a wallet, brown, with a Gucci symbol on it, and a small belt holding it together, must be the dead guy's wallet, Nyx thought her head still racing, it had blood on it.

She bent down and picked it up, as her knees cracked, the sweat on her palms dripping. She opened the wallet with caution, trying not to touch the blood. She pulled out the driving license, squinting her eyes to read the name, after giving up on looking at the picture that was scratched off, weird. She rubbed her eyes with her sweaty palms. Ryan Edin.

It was her dad.

'Fuck. Fuck. FUCK. NO'. Nyx's hands were stained with blood, she closed her mouth, her muddy fingernails piercing into her cheeks, she stumbled back and screamed. Dexter came running in, panting.

'Nyx are you OK?' he asked, as he held his legs gasping for air.

She did not hear him, she heard a gun, it was in her mind. Nyx's heart shattered as she realized the truth - her father was dead. The shock and grief washed over her in waves, leaving her numb and speechless. Tears streamed down her face as she knelt down, crying. Her palms now filled with tears.

Dex saw the picture in her hands.

'My dad, he-' Nyx tried to say, but she heard another gunshot, again, not real. It was in her mind.

Dex understood and sat next to her, hugging her cold body, trying to comfort it. She clutched the wallet tightly in her hand. The image of his smiling face in the picture burned into her memory, a painful reminder of the man she had loved and lost. 'I never fucking said goodbye Dex-' she cried. Dex held her hand, nodding. Nyx's tears flowed freely, the weight of the loss crushing her spirit. Each sob wracked her body, the pain of her sorrow overwhelming her senses.

She didn't try to hold back the tears, her head hurt, it pierced with pain ......Boom. She heard a gunshot.

Nyx's sobs echoed through the empty warehouse, the sound of her grief filling the air. With each sob, Nyx felt a flood of memories wash over her - moments shared with her father, laughter and love intertwined with the pain of his absence. Nyx felt angry, her own mother, her own fucking blood had killed her dad. But why?

Nyx got up, 'Dex, let's go'……. Boom. Another shot.

Dex looked at her worried,' Nyx, I-'

'Let's go, I can't be here' she said, as she tucked the bloody wallet into her pocket and walked outside to her cycle. The gunshots echoing in her ears.

The drive back was sad and felt heavy as if they were carrying the body back with them, Nyx was still shedding tears. She had never felt this before. She felt weak. When they were out of the woods, she looked over at Dex 'Go home, it's late, Bye.'

'Are you going to be, OK? I can stay-' 'It's fine, go home.'

Dex nodded and side-hugged her from his cycle, then drove off. Nyx got off her cycle and walked over to her house. She went inside and saw her mom sitting on the couch, filling her nails.

'You're back early Nyx' Alicia said looking up at her.

'Yeah,' Nyx said. She went up to her room and laid on her bed. She had to.

Boom, another gunshot went off in her head.

# Chapter – 12

Nyx could not see her mom without thinking of the gunshot. It broke her, her soul. She could not sleep, her head hurt, her ears hurt. She heard gunshots in her mind, she had to get revenge on Alicia Ada. But how? She was alone.

She needed help.

She texted him "Hi" and waited. Dex replied "I'm outside your house right now."

Of course, he was, she smiled. Nyx jumped off her chair and walked downstairs, the creaking of the stairs made her shiver, it sounded like the floorboards creaking in the warehouse when her dad had died. She saw Dex through the big glass window. He jumped around trying to avoid a bee flying around him. A maid opened the door.

'Oh, thank you' he said shooing away the bee, getting in as fast as he could.

'Hey' Nyx said as she scratched the back of her arm, trying to itch the pain away.

'I hope you didn't see that, you know, me and that fucking bee, let's pretend that never happened.'

'I was going to explore Mom's office in a couple of minutes, she's not home right now. You know to find clues about what she's doing and why she killed Dad,' she sighed pulling herself together.

'Oh, yeah, I can help.'

They walked inside. Nyx knew the room was off-limits, ever since she was a kid, even when her dad was around, Alicia would scream at her when she went near that office, Nyx never cared, but now, now she did.

It was on the third floor of the mansion, in the corner, with a padlock. Nyx had spied on her mom the day before. She needed revenge. As they walked up the grand staircase, Dex looked around, 'Where are all the staff?' he asked trying to fix his hair.

'We are having a party; they are working in the backyard.' She heard another gunshot go of in her mind, she held her arm up to her head, trying not to think.

'Oh, why a party?'

'My mom's throwing a birthday party for her sister' Nyx said as she walked over to the office, trying to shoo away the thoughts in her mind. She was going crazy.

She clicked on the password- 160309, she heard another gunshot go off in her head. It was like a rhythm.

They were in.

As Nyx and Dexter sift through the documents in the off-limits room, they come across incriminating evidence that reveals Nyx's mom's involvement in illegal activities. She grabbed a stack of papers, with a list of names, and a red cross on each face. 'Wait-' she said looking at a man's face, 'Dex, isn't he the recent victim of the slasher?'

'Hey, wait, it is, his name, Umm, I forgot-' he said scratching his neck.

'Dave. Dave Rao?' she mumbled, looking up at him. Her fingers glided across the files, as she scanned them for details.

'Yes, him!'

'My Mom killed him, and skinned him, and hung his skin on a tree.' she whispered, her voice trembling, as she shook the files.

'Why?'

'I don't know, but this may be a clue, we need to find out more about him.'

'Dave Rao, a former police officer renowned for his expertise in apprehending criminals, made a significant impact on public safety throughout his career. He prevented a potentially catastrophic incident at The City Mall, by stopping an individual named Liam Ohm from carrying out a drug ring, saving countless lives in the process. May his dedicated service and courageous actions be remembered, as we honor his memory and legacy' Dexter read out from a newspaper clipping that slid out from the file.

There was another paper, that had the heading "Employee X4 Liam Ohm."

'Liam Ohm?' Nyx recalled, she scratched her chin, trying to figure out who it was. Liam Ohm. Where did she hear that? Liam Ohm. Think Nyx. Think, the name echoed in her thought.

'You know him?' Dex asked, breaking Nyx from her thoughts. 'Wait, I do-' her eyes glinted.

'Max, Max Ohm!'

'How is he related to Liam?'

Nyx cut him off, 'Max, he goes to my class, his brother, Liam, he's in jail, it's the same person, I'm sure.'

'OK', Dex looked confused.

'I can ask Max about him, Liam might have worked for my mom, and Max must know something about Liam's arrest and Dave Rao's death. '

She put the papers down and looked up at the board hung on the wall, there were more newspaper clippings held up by pins.

"Drug Ring Exposed: Multiple Arrests Made", "Drug Trafficking Network Uncovered", "Meth Bags found in abandoned House."

Nyx gasped. Her heart raced, as she realized the extent of her mother's involvement in the criminal underworld. The newspaper clippings on the board painted a vivid picture of a powerful drug empire that her mother controlled.

She was more than that, she was also a fucking murderer.

The headlines spoke of arrests, drug trafficking networks, and meth bags found in abandoned houses - all linked to Nyx's mother, as the mastermind behind it all, but no one knew, it was Alicia Ada.

Dexter walked over and stared at the board. He read the headlines wide-eyed.

Nyx looked over at him, he was freaked out. She wanted to expose her mother, but how? She picked up a pen, but it fell to the floor, her sweaty palms gave out. She heard another gun shot in her head. Why was she imaging all this. Nyx, focus, she whispered, moving away.

She began gathering evidence from the hidden room, including incriminating documents, photos, and any other information that could link her mother, to the drug trafficking network and all the murders. She had to destroy her mom. Nyx created an anonymous email account and sent the evidence to herself.

Nyx and Dexter decided to handle the situation on their own, without involving the authorities. They knew that going to the police could lead to a dangerous confrontation and potentially put their lives at risk. They had to stop this drug ring by themselves. Even if they wanted the police to help, there was no chance they would, Alicia would do something, Nyx had to do it herself.

She logged into Mail on the laptop, and started creating a new account, Dex leaned over 'Whatchya making?' he asked pushing the chair, 'A fake ID, to send all the files over to me.'

'Smart, wait, how did you know the password for the laptop? 'Same as the one we used to get in.'

'Smart, again, not your mom, you.'

'Please enter your New Mail ID' Nyx read out, as she typed it in-

'haychtu@mail.com' she mumbled, 'What does "haychtu" mean?' Dex asked to read it over and over. 'I don't know.'

She uploaded all the files This had just begun.

They tore through all the cabinets in the hidden room, searching for any incriminating evidence that could expose Nyx's mother's illegal activities. They rummaged through files, documents, and storage boxes.

After tearing through all the cabinets and gathering the incriminating evidence, Nyx and Dexter meticulously cleaned up the hidden room, making sure to leave no trace of their presence behind. They carefully replaced the files, documents, and storage boxes exactly as they had found them, ensuring everything appeared undisturbed. Nyx locked the door and they walked off.

Nyx slammed her door after Dexter walked in, they shuddered, why was it so cold? She sat on the bed gathering all the evidence. She looked over at Dexter, who was scanning a QR code that was on a file. 'It's a coupon for 44 bags of baby powder.' He giggled, looking over at her.

'What?!' Laughed Nyx, as she zipped up her jacket 'Wait. It can't be baby powder, it's probably-' 'Drugs.' finished Nyx.

She sighed. What could she do? 'Well Mom's coming home early, there's a party, remember?'

'Oh, yeah, then Imma head home' Dex said putting the files down 'You should come later, to the party.'

'I'll try, Bye' 'Bye Dex.'

Dexter closed the door and walked down the stairs. He saw Alicia's car pulling up.

Her heels clicked as she got out.

# Chapter – 13

As the sun began to set, casting a warm glow over the garden, Nyx stood before her mirror, admiring her reflection in the soft light. She wore her best dress, a flowing emerald green gown that sparkled with sequins and beads. The sound of laughter and music drifted in from the garden, where the party was in full swing. Alicia was chatting away with friends, and her aunt, the birthday girl, was dancing. She kept on hearing the gunshot over and over and over.

Sarah was her aunt, thirty but could pass as a twenty-year-old. She was a vision of beauty, with her long, flowing hair, cascading down her back and her radiant smile lighting up the night. Despite being thirty, she had a timeless elegance and grace that made her look much younger. Nyx walked down to the garden; her heart felt heavy. She could not look at her mom the same way again. She tried to avoid her and walked over to her aunt

She walked over to Sarah trying to muster a smile to match the festive atmosphere outside. Despite the enchanting glow of the setting sun and the lively sounds of laughter and music, a cloud of unease lingered over her. Her mom was a drug dealer. A murderer. A bitch.

As Nyx stood during the party, her eyes scanned the garden in anticipation of Dexter's arrival. He was never late, like her. She looked around once more, before texting him. No reply. Nyx was worried, so she ran outside and called him, getting away from the music.

'Hello?'

'Nyx, hey' 'Where are you?'

'Don't get mad' 'What?'

'I'm in the woods, I'm trying to find more clues on why your mom killed your dad.'

'Dexter! It's 8 P.M., get out of there, oh god.'

'Fine.'

'Stop by over here, I'll get you some cake' 'Yeah, Bye.'

Dexter stood in the middle of the warehouse, as he cut the call. Weird. Cell service in the middle of nowhere. He decided to explore a little more before going back, he put his phone in his pocket and held onto a bat he had grabbed from home. Come on, don't judge him, he was scared.

Dex walked towards a small door in the warehouse and put his ear up to the door.

There was a muffling sound. 'What the-' Dex stepped back, holding the bat up.

Suddenly it got worse, the sound grew louder. At first, the sound was indistinct, a low murmur that sent a shiver down his spine. But then, to his horror, the muffled noise intensified, growing louder and more frantic with each passing second...

Dexter's heart raced; he stepped back and ran. Reaching the door leading outside, he flung it open and dashed into the cool night air. His breath came in ragged gasps as he made a beeline for his cycle. He had millions of thoughts going on in his head, he dropped the bat and jumped onto his cycle, kicking off the stone holding the wheel.

What if Alicia had left someone there? Maybe a hostage? He had to tell Nyx.

He peddled hard out of the forest, sweating, he made a quick turn towards Nyx's house and drove towards the driveway, he dropped his cycle and ran towards Nyx, who was standing, looking at her phone, holding a box of cake.

'NYX' he screamed.

'God, what?' she said, startled, looking at Dexter.

'I heard something in the warehouse, it was like a low murmur, someone is in there' he stammered, still panting, wiping his face on his shirt.

'It can't be my dad, I saw him die in front of me, I heard the gun shoot through his soul' she whispered gripping onto the box.

'Nyx, I know, but there is someone in there.'

'Ok...we'll figure it out, thanks for helping me, Dex. Here, take this home.'

'Finally, something that will calm me down' Dex smiled taking the box filled with cake.

'Bye, I gotta go back inside' Nyx said.

'Bye, thanks for the cake, also, Max, don't forget to ask him about his brother, Liam' 'right, I will.'

Nyx walked back inside. Could her mom really be holding someone hostage? Or was it security? She shook her head in confusion and she lifted her phone, as she got a message.

TO-nyxtheada@mail.com FROM-r4455@mail.com

I know what happened, I know. Not safe Nyx. Alicia would kill you. Try not to get caught. Just stop. It's not safe. Please. I care.

She gasped; it had been a while since she had got a message. Would her own Mom kill her, just to keep the "business" under cover? Nyx put her phone inside her pocket and went back to the party. And what did r4455 mean by "I care"?

She grabbed her Air Pods and put them in her ears, she had to block out the loud sounds. And the gunshot replaying in her ears.

"Make You Mine" by Madison Beer played in her ears as she walked past all the people. The music drowned out the noise of the party, and the gunshot echoes, as she tried to think.

"I, I, I wanna lay, lay, lay, Wanna string, string, string, Wanna Make you mine" The music in her Air Pods guided her movements, she ran through all the people, she saw her mom from the side of her eye, drunk. Nyx saw the swimming pool, which was closed and empty. Perfect.

As she reached the edge of the pool, Nyx paused for a moment, the music still playing in her ears. With a deep breath, she took a leap of faith and jumped into the empty pool, the rush of adrenaline coursing through her veins. She swam up to the edge looking down at the view. Yes. She was still in her party dress. The green crystals sparkled in the water. The water sparkled with the reflection of the moonlight, casting a mesmerizing glow over the pool.

The chaos and what Dexter told her did not bother her, Nyx couldn't help but feel a sense of peace, as she floated in the water, the music in her ears serving as a comforting soundtrack to her moment of solitude. She got up and pushed herself onto the side. Nyx's hair glistened in the dim light, her wet hair cascading down her back in dark waves. As she emerged from the pool, droplets of water clung to her dress, highlighting every crystal. 'Why did I do that?' she laughed as she shook out her hair.

She did not hear the gunshots anymore. She heard a voice in her head saying revenge.

R    e    v    e    n    g    e

# Chapter – 14

Nyx stood by her bed as her phone rang. She was calling Max Ohm; she got his number from the school register. The phone rang, as Nyx held her breath. Maybe he knew something, big or small, he had to help her.

'Hello?' a cold voice answered the phone 'Hello, Is this?'

'Do I know you?'

'Umm, I'm Nyx, from your class, I was wondering if you could.'

'Nyx? Nyx Ada?'

'Yes' (sigh) 'I'm Nyx Ada, from the 11th grade s-' 'Yeah, yeah, I know you.'

'You are Max right...Max Ohm?'

'Mhm, go on, what do you want? Oh, for fucks sake, don't tell me we have a project due.'

'No, no, that's not it, I was wondering' 'Go on.'

'Your brother, Liam' 'What about Liam?'

'Umm, did he have a job, when he was arrested?'

'Uh, yeah, he worked for someone, I don't know who. She paid him well, he told me that all the time, but he got caught, and he won't tell who got him involved in the drug ring scandal.'

'OK, interesting.'

'Why the fuck are you asking?' 'I, I umm, wanted to know' 'OK?'

'Also, did he ever say if he worked for a particular company?' 'No, he never said, it's like he worked in some gang, Haha.'

'Haha, quick question, he was arrested and caught by Dave Rao, the officer, right?'

'I guess it was him, he died right, that son of a…' 'Yes, he did die.'

'OK, well, do you need to "interrogate" me more?' 'Oh, umm, that's all, Thank you.'

'OK, Bye Nyx.'

She hung up. Her mom killed him. That bitch, she killed Dave Rao.

'Where were you all night Nyx?' Alicia walked into Nyx's room, scaring the crap out of her.

Nyx jumped up, and turned her phone off as she walked over to the windows.

She opened the curtains, and the sun shone into the room. Alicia hissed, as she stepped back when the sunlight hit her face. 'I was in the pool' Nyx said, looking bored, her black hair covering her eyes.

'Fully clothed?' her eyes shot up from her coffee mug 'Yes.'

She rolled her eyes and walked away from the bright room. Nyx looked up 'Mom.'

Alicia turned around swiftly, her eyes still adjusting to the light, 'What?'

'In the woods, behind our house, we have a warehouse, right?' Nyx asked, looking at Alicia.

Alicia looked down at her cup 'Yes. "We" don't have it. "I" have it' That Bitch- How the fuck could she say that- She……..

Calm down Nyx

Nyx nodded, biting her lip, watching a murderer, I mean- mother, walk away.

Nyx smiled slyly. She went over to her window, which had a view of the woods, with gnarled trees stretching and twisting around towards the sky. Thick undergrowth choked the forest floor, hiding the pathway.

Her sly smile widened, as she looked out into the creepy woods from her room window. She was going to destroy her mom's life. How? She had to think.

Her heart skipped a beat as she noticed the flashing lights of police cars in the distance, their red and blue hues. She watched as the police cars parked near the forest's edge, their headlights illuminating the trees and casting long shadows on the ground. She could see officers moving quickly, their flashlights scanning the area, as they searched for something- or someone.

Her dad. He was missing, he was dead. Only she knew it. She had to go. This was her chance, to expose her mom

She went down grabbed her cycle and drove over to the woods, every second she peddled, she thought about what to say "OFFICERS, MY MOTHER IS A MURDER" no, she can't say that, how about "OFFICERS THE DEAD GUY, IS MY DAD, MY MOTHER, SHE SHOT HIM" no. Fuck, how could she tell them, she slowed down as she reached the entrance of the woods, her fingers gripped onto the cycle, as she walked over to the Police car. She noticed the officers looking over at her.

'Sorry, we can't let anyone in' an officer said, holding up his hand, his sunglasses reflecting Nyx's image on it.

She nodded, stopping her cycle, 'I live there, thought I could help.' she said pointing over to her house.

'Do you see anyone going in here' the officer asked taking his glasses off.

'I saw a black car, two, going in and out. Bad news. You should really look into it, Officer,' Nyx said, squinting her eyes at him. Come on, come on, she thought.

A police officer came running out from the woods with a flashlight, his eyes red, and sweat pouring from the sides of his forehead.

'Slasher strikes again' he gasped, holding his knees as he panted. 'I saw skin hanging on the trees.'

Nyx gasped. Was her mom "The Slasher" who killed people and hung their skins on trees.

So, it was true. Her mom was the slasher. She killed anyone who tried to come in her way.

Nyx held her jacket, that she had taken off, as her palms got sweaty. Again. The gunshot went off in her mind.

Wait, the skin was-

Alicia Ada had hung Ryan Edin's skin, it had to be his?

It was her dad's. Nyx looked wide-eyed as her ears replayed the gunshot she heard, she ran back with her cycle in her hand, the wheels screeching on the road. She fell onto the curb of her house, crying.

Her sobs wracked her body, the tears fell onto her phone. Her ears were ringing as she cried. Each sob tore through her like a knife, reopening wounds that she never knew existed. She felt a flicker of anger rise within her. She got up and ran into her house. She had to deal with that bitch. Alicia Ada.

Alicia was standing in the kitchen, as the chef recited the Menu for the month Nyx could not see her mom, she saw a fucking killer. She walked over and grabbed the knife from the chef's apron, pushed her mom, and pointed the knife at her throat. 'Your skin would look beautiful hung on a tree' She screamed, as her tears poured through. Her voice was a venomous snarl. The knife trembled in her hand, her finger gripping tighter onto it, as her palms got sweatier. The chef screamed and called for help. 'Oh, shut up' Nyx hissed.

'NYX, what the fuck are you doing?' her mom whispered looking at the knife, her eyes wide open. Sweat poured down her face. If she moved even an inch, the knife would slice her, the blood would pour out, staining her beautiful dress.

Nyx smiled, she felt a rush of excitement, she understood why her mom loved killing. 'Doesn't feel good when you're on the other side?' she asked her mom tilting her head, sarcastically.

'I don't know what you're talking about-' Alicia dropped her phone to the ground.

Boom, it shattered.

No, Nyx, NO, you can't hear the gunshot again, it's just your mind. She closed her eyes, pushing the sound away.

The guards ran in grabbing Nyx's hand, which made her drop the knife. Alicia got up, gasping for air, clutching onto her stomach. 'TAKE THAT BITCH TO THE FUCKING INSANE ASYLUM.'

Nyx tried pull away, from the guards reaching for the knife. The voice in her head said "Revenge."

'YOU BITCH, YOU WANT TO KILL ME.' Alicia screamed as the maids helped her calm down.

"Revenge" the voice hissed.

Nyx smiled, as she was dragged away by the guards. She could hear her.

Mom screaming at her. She actually couldn't hear it. She closed her eyes. She heard sirens. But she could not open her eyes. She closed her mouth and listened to her head.

The voice hissed again.

R  e  v  e  n  g  e   She had to take it.

# Chapter – 15

Alicia Ada looked out the huge balcony from her office. The funeral was over and she had come home exhausted. She was tired of everything, dealing with her business, having to shut people up after they saw the shit she did, and dealing with assholes. But she was making money cause of this. She was rich, she was self-made, and no man helped her get up here, not even Ryan, her Ex. It was all her's. She was selfish as fuck, of course.

Alicia turned around and walked over to the small bookcase in the corner of the room, a sense of anticipation filled the air. Her fingers traced the spines of the books until they landed on one, with red lace.

Without hesitation, she pulled it out, revealing a hidden door. Alicia gracefully went in as her purple dress dragged behind her, a network of corridors snaked underneath the huge mansion, it was dimly lit. These corridors were not just empty passageways; they were filled with secrets, danger, and the illicit activities that Alicia was involved in. She walked further in and walked over to a tattered door that had a sign- LOT 15.

She kicked open the door with her red stilettos, the heel fell to the floor.

A frail man was sitting in the corner, holding up his hand to his eyes as a small amount of light entered the dark room. He was injured and had bruises, he looked up at Alicia with a mixture of fear and anger and picked up the heel handing it to her, seeing the look on her face.

'What do you want?' he asked getting up, holding his bruised arm, 'You to die' Alicia said, as she bent down putting her heel back on. 'Kill me then.'

'I still have to get more shit out of you' she replied, rubbing her ankle.

'What' he asked

'My guards will be coming later, dear, I just came to tell you so that you could prepare your frail ass' Alicia said stepping in.

Alicia smiled looking at him. She pulled out a knife and crouched down.

'You know that bitch, Nyx, she tried killing me with this knife' she said showing him the knife.

'Good girl' he said looking away.

Alicia extended her hand with the knife and sliced his hand. The blood splattered on her face. He screeched as he pulled his hand in. She giggled and got up, slamming the door behind her. What a weak ass, she thought, can't even handle a little pain.

Nyx waited outside the office. She kept on knocking, but the door was locked, and she knew Alicia was inside.

'Mom?' she called.

She heard something, and the door flew open.

'Mom, can you tell the chef I don't want-' she said as she looked up from her phone.

Nyx stopped; she saw the red stuff on her mom's face 'What is that' she asked stepping back.

'My pen leaked, and it splattered on my face' Alicia's hand in her purse, as she rummaged for a tissue, she quickly grabbed a crumpled- up tissue and ran it over her face. 'You can go now Nyx.'

'OK? Tell the chef I won't be there for dinner', she said. 'OK.'

Nyx walked off; she knew it was not ink. She could smell something copperish. It was blood. She had smelt it on her dad's wallet. The smell stuck with her. It was embedded within her. Forever.

She had to explore the office. But how could Alicia kill someone in that office, Nyx turned around to take a peek, but the door was already locked. She sighed. Her Mom loved lying. And she was good at it. Maybe she had just killed someone in there. What a psychopath, I mean, Nyx also nearly killed.

Her mom, she did have it in her blood, you know the manic blood. She wanted to strangle her and see the pain. She wanted to feel the excitement again, the rush she felt when she held the knife to her throat. It was beautiful. The pain in someone's eyes is beautiful.

Gosh, she was also like her mom. I thought Nyx would be the good kid with a psychotic Mom, but she was the same.

# Chapter – 16

Nyx and Alicia were heading out to an event, again. They locked up and left. The maids, chefs, and butlers left. The guards stood out keeping watch. It was 8:30.

Alicia had locked her office as usual.

The man slowly crept out from his hiding place in the room, he made his way to the door. He had a pin with him. Alicia had dropped it after she cut his hand.

He turned the pin, which opened the door. 'Phew' he sighed. He grabbed a lipstick on the table.

He walked through the office. He had to let people know he was in there, but he could not escape, the guards surrounded the property, and if he tried, he would die. The man slowly picked the lock on the door and got out. He walked over to Nyx's room.

Nyx was chatting away with friends in the event. She had not met them in a long time. Nyx realized it was getting late, and she walked around trying to find her mom. Her phone buzzed with a notification.

FROM-r4455@mail.com TO-nyxtheada@mail.com

Come home, now. Or it will go up in flames.

Nyx gasped, What the fuck, she ran to her mom and showed her the message.

Alicia rolled her eyes 'God, someone is messing around, even if our house burns, I have ten more mansions around the city.'

Nyx shook her head in sarcasm, 'I'm going home.'

She went out and booked a taxi, while waiting she texted Dexter to come over.

As soon as the taxi stopped in front of her house, Nyx got up and ran to her house, the guards opened the door, and Dex was waiting for her.

'Hey Nyx' Dexter said, as he walked over.

'Hey, look at this' she said, showing him the text.

'Well, let's go in before your house burns down.'

They walked in after the guard unlocked the door. 'Woah, no maids or butlers in here' Dex said, looking around at the empty place.

Nyx looked around slowly and walked up to her room, nothing weird. 'Uh, another prank?' she said, collapsing on her bed. She was sick of it. Who was r4455?

'Yup' Dex said, as he played some music on his phone.

'Fuck it, I'm going to wash my face, that event was so crappy and I'm tired' she said walking to her bathroom.

Dex bobbed his head to the music.

Nyx walked in and looked at herself in the mirror. 'fuck' she fell to the floor and started screaming. Dex pushed open the door.

He saw Nyx on the floor, she looked whiter than a ghost. 'What?' he asked.

Nyx looked up, and her frail finger pointed at the mirror HELP ME, NYX.

'What the fuck' Dex said walking over to the mirror.

'Someone is in here Dexter' Nyx said getting up.

Nyx dragged Dexter out and locked the bathroom from outside. 'They wrote it with lipstick' he said.

'That color is the one my mom uses. But she can't be doing this, because it was not there when we left from here, can't be the guards, whenever someone enters the house we get a notification, look' she said pointing her phone to him, the only message she got was the one from r4455 and since she and Dex had come in, there was a notification.

'So, someone is trapped in here?' Dex asked looking around scared.

Nyx nodded. 'Maybe my mom has a prison for the people who try to expose her business?'

The man slowly closed the door, returning to the room he was locked up in. He left a note for Nyx. She had to see it. He crouched down and pulled up a small blanket he had as he tossed aside the lipstick. He sat there in silence, hoping Nyx would help him. She was his only and last hope.

# Chapter – 17

Riley opened her eyes. She rolled around in bed, the small room lit up with the light from the hallway. Her hair was in a messy bun, she grabbed her phone and it was 11:00. She always woke up late. She kicked off her sheets and got out heading into the tiny bathroom. The shower was already turned on for her.

She stepped in washing her long hair, as she listened to her playlist play on her phone, the soapy water drained as she stood under the cascading water. The water stopped. 'Not again' Riley sighed as she stood on her heels fixing the shower head that dripped slowly, her hand slowly slid down the rod she noticed a large bug on her hand, she shrugged it off as she got out of the shower, grabbing her towel.

She sat on the couch drying her hair when she got a text from Nyx. NYX- Hey, we should hang out again. Why don't you come home? RILEY- Hey, Sup? I'll come over later.

She tossed her phone aside, letting the couch swallow her, she felt tired. Her eyes fluttering, as she tried to open them

Simon walked in, 'Hey Riley, I'm heading out, Mom said she doesn't want to cook, and she asked me to get food. What do you want?'

'Can you get me sushi?' 'For breakfast? Alright.'

Riley nodded as she walked over to lock the door. 'Oh, for fucks sake' she fell hard and hit her head on the floor. She just fainted but came again. What the fuck was going on, she stood up and walked over to the only bathroom, and knocked 'MOM.'

'Yes, Riley' her mom said turning off the shower 'I think I fainted.'

'WHAT, WAIT I'M COMING HONEY.'

Overprotective Moms. Am I right? It's even worse if they spoil their kids rotten. 'OH GOD, HONEY, ARE YOU OK?'

'Yes. I fell.'

Her Mom dragged her to the couch and sat her down 'I'm booking an appointment with your doctor.'

'Mom, you don't-' 'KEEP QUIET.'

Riley sighed as she leaned on the stained white wall, her back cracking.

'Hello? Yes, It's Mrs. Simon, yes, Mother of Riley Simons. I want to book an urgent appointment for her, yes,' she spoke in a worried voice 'She fainted and I think she's sick, yes.'

Riley looked at her mom as she got up, to go and get dressed 'Go get dressed dear, I'll tell your dad.'

The door swung open, and Simon was standing in the doorway with the food, 'What happened?' he asked looking at his wife, who looked freaked out.

'OH DEAR, she fainted near the doorway, and look at her she looks so sick.'

Well, it was true, Riley looked tired, she was probably just tired, worn out by all the singing lessons.

Simon walked over and sat next to her 'Calm down Patricia. Some food should help her' he handed Riley the box of sushi. 'Eat this, Riley.'

Riley reached over for the food and grabbed a piece, she put it in her mouth and chewed. It tasted disgusting, but she loved sushi more than anything. She threw up, vomiting all over the small table. Simon looked horrified, the vomit was red. Riley started crying, and then she fell on her dad, vomit still coming out of her mouth.

Nyx stood waiting for Riley to reply to her texts, as the thunder clouds surrounded the neighborhood, where was she?

NYX- Hey Riley, you said you're coming over? NYX- Riley? Are you there?

NYX- You are always online, everything OK? NYX- Riley?

Nyx looked at her watch, as her driver stopped in front of the apartment. Riley was not responding to her texts, she was worried, Nyx walked in, and went in, she rang the bell. But no one opened the door. She stood there knowing they might be sleeping, when a neighbor opened the door. 'Hi, Dear. They are not home'

'Where are they? My friend is not replying to my texts, and not lifting the-' 'In the hospital. Your friend must be Riley.'

'Yes, what happened?'

'She was unconscious, the paramedics had come, and she was throwing up blood. Poor thing, she was pale and looked so tired.'

Nyx's heart raced, as she heard the news about her friend Riley.

'Which hospital are they at?' Nyx asked as she put her phone to her ear, ringing Simon.

'The one near 5th avenue' 'OK.'

Nyx raced down the stairs as she hung up the call. No one was lifting their calls, she went into her car and noticed her driver was standing in the corner smoking, Nyx made a split-second decision and got behind the wheel herself.

Her heart pounded in her chest as she raced towards the hospital, the sound of the engine roaring in her ears. The city streets blurred past in a dizzying whirlwind of lights and colors as she weaved in and out of traffic, her foot pressing down hard on the accelerator. Her knuckles were white as she gripped the steering wheel, as sweat dripped down her neck. Cars honked and swerved out of her way as Nyx pushed the speed limit to its breaking point, the adrenaline coursing through her green veins.

But why did she care so much? She hated Riley, didn't she?

As she screeched to a halt in front of the emergency entrance, Nyx's heart was pounding in her chest, her breath coming in short, ragged gasps. She flew out of the car, her feet pounding against the pavement as she sprinted towards the entrance. A nurse walked past her 'Everything OK?' she asked looked at Nyx.

'Is Riley here? Riley Simons?'

The nurse pulled up her chart, as she tucked the pen into her pocket 'Yes. Room 345.'

'OK.'

'Wait, you can't go in yet. The doctor just got her tests back, he needs to speak with them, you can wait here' she said, pointing towards the waiting room.

Nyx nodded and went in.

# Chapter – 18

Nyx knocked on the door, and a nurse opened it. 'Riley is eating dear, but you can come in' she said closing the door after she walked in.

Nyx walked in and saw Riley drinking soup; her eyes were red and her skin frail 'Hey'. Riley looked up 'Oh. Hi, come sit. Mom and Dad are down, discussing something' Nyx nodded as she sat next to her. 'What happened, you were not replying to my texts, I tried to call you, and your dad, but no one picked up, I asked your neighbor, and she said you were throwing up and I.'

'I have skin cancer.'

Nyx's eyes widened 'What?' her hands holding onto Riley's to comfort her. 'Got diagnosed today, stage three, I may die, Nyx' she said, trying not to cry, 'Hey, you won't, I know you won't' her hand holding on even tighter.'

Riley looked up at her 'My parents have no money Nyx, I will die.' 'Look at me, you won't, OK? I'll ask my mom to help your dad.' 'She hates him Nyx.'

'Then I will steal money from her and send it over. OK.'

Riley giggled as she put the bowl of soup down. 'You are really nice, except when you called me a bitch', Nyx laughed as she tucked a strand of Riley's hair back.

'All of this will be gone I guess, my hair,' Riley said, pushing her hair back. 'It will grow back, and you will look better than ever.'

'I might not be able to sing again. If I die.' 'Riley, you will get better, don't say that.'

'Fuck it, I should have known my tiredness was getting a little too much, I should have told someone, instead I shut up, I could have been saved Nyx.'

Riley felt the pang of vomit hit her again, she turned to the side and threw up, the red blood splattering all over the cold white marble tiles, Nyx held onto her and called for the nurse, she saw the blood and closed her eyes. The wallet. She shook off her thoughts and comforted Riley as the nurse handed her tissues and started cleaning up the mess. The white sheets were now red. and Nyx teared up. It reminded her of the gunshot, the blood on the floor, and his wallet, the memories were coming back.

'You should go back Nyx.' Riley said, as she wiped her mouth, her hand stained with red vomit, her fingernails dug into her cheeks as she scrapped her skin.

'OK, but please take care. You will make it, tell me if I have to "steal" money from my mom' Nyx said, letting go slowly.

'Haha, OK, bye Nyx' Riley said, as she held her stomach in pain 'Bye pretty.'

Nyx closed the door behind her and sighed. She could not lose another person. She looked into her phone. 5 missed calls from Dexter.

She rang him as soon as she was out of the hospital 'Hey Dexter, I was in the hospital.'

'Why, are you OK?'

'It's Riley, she has cancer' 'WHAT, is she OK?'

'Not really, but she has a little hope' 'Good. Well, I got a message from r4455' 'What was it?'

'Go to the warehouse.'

# Chapter – 19

'Are you sure we should do this?' Dex said pushing his hair back, as he hid behind the warehouse.

'Yes Dex. We are finally going to see r4455' she sighed, kicking a stick away from her.

'But it's 8:00, and dark, and the message said to come at 8:00, but he is not here yet' Dexter said, as he took off his jacket handing it to Nyx, who was shivering.

'Wait' she said.

'Yeah?'

'What if the text did not mean, go there, I'm going to be there. What if it meant, searching the warehouse? Like it asked us to come here, it does not mean we are meeting up with that person, right?'

'Yes, makes sense, so, are we going in?' he said looking around 'Yes.'

'Nyx, but can you? Last time you.'

'It's fine. I'm going' She cut him off. She was going to enter the same place where she saw blood. Her dad's blood.

Dexter nodded and followed her in, he noticed a shift in her expression when she stepped in. She was not OK.

They looked around slowly, walking around in caution. Nyx stopped and looked down at the place, where she found her dad's wallet, where he died. She saw blood. Blood everywhere, there wasn't any on the floor, she was imagining it. How could Alicia?

Dex walked over and held her hand 'Come on, let's go' breaking her away from her thoughts.

Nyx nodded and they walked away from there, she walked over to a mirror and looked in it, Dex was behind her, looking into a small cabinet, with red and white paint 'Nyx, check this out' he said holding up a paper. 'It's a number' 20030814109.

'Wait. Let's call it' she said taking out her phone.

The wind was getting worse outside, and the trees rustled, the sound was spooky. She dialed in the number and stood in silence.

Nyx put the phone on speaker, as it rang.

They waited anxiously as the phone continued to ring, Nyx's heart pounding in her chest. Finally, after what felt like an eternity, the other person picked up.

'What the!' Dex said in surprise, as Nyx shushed him 'Hello?' She spoke...

'Hi Nyx' A male voice replied 'Umm...who are you?'

'Can't tell dear. You might-' he stopped.

'I see you found my number. You should have known by now. I'm r4455' 'Are you Simon?' she asked holding her breath.

There was a chuckle on the other side 'No.'

'Why are you messaging us?'

'You need to know the truth Nyx, please, help me.' 'Where are you?'

'In your mansion. Under it to be exact' 'WHAT!'

'Yes-I-Hello?' 'Hello?'

The call was cut. 'He- he, he's in my house' she stuttered.

'It's going to be OK, Nyx, we will help him, I think your mom might have done something to him' he said.

'Maybe. Oh my god. I hate her so much; I wish I killed her when I got the chance.'

'Nyx, let's go home.'

# Chapter – 20

Dexter sat on Nyx's bed, while she stood near the window looking out at the woods.

'I don't know what to do, how do I help that guy? Where are the weird tunnels under my house?'

'We will find it Nyx; you're stressing a lot' Dex said, getting up and walking over. 'Of course, I will stress, I'm living in the same house, with a bitch who

killed my dad, and some dude is texting me asking to help him and something and Riley is sick.'

'Hey, it's OK, and you should check on Riley...' he said tossing her phone.

'Yeah, I'll call her later' replied Nyx holding her forehead.

Dex got up and walked over to her 'Well, I'm going to go home, my grandma is coming home.'

'Ok, bye, tell her I said hi' Dex nodded and went out.

Nyx stood and looked out the window when she heard a hissing sound. 'Dex-' she said, turning around. She turned and saw a man, not Dexter. He was wearing a black mask and his face was covered in bruises. Nyx gasped and stepped back, hiding her phone from his view.

'Throw that down' he barked, his voice was raspy and weird like he was faking it. He was tall and had blonde, dirty, matted hair.

Nyx slid her phone down.

'Please, don't hurt me' she begged; Nyx's heart pounded in her chest.

'I won't hurt you, dear. I will hurt your mom. I'm locking you in your room, stay here, don't scream.'

'What!'

The man stormed out slamming the door. And she heard it lock from the outside, Nyx ran and put her ear up to the door, trying to figure out where he was going. Shit. She heard her mom come in through the main door, she was going to die.

Nyx slid down, I mean, her mom deserved it, she probably tried to kill this man, and he was just trying to get revenge. Nyx sat there in silence, she smirked. She wanted her mom to get hurt, she deserved it.

The man stood on the top of the staircase, looking down as Alicia walked in. 'Hello Alicia' he shouted.

She looked up. She knew that he had escaped, she looked out, about to call the guards.

'Oh, you look scared, do you always need your guards to save you?' he said climbing down.

She laughed 'Looks like the dog escaped from its cage. Go back you mutt' 'I'm going to kill you now' he said pulling out a knife.

'That's mine, you stole it you rat' 'I thought I was a dog?'

Alicia pulled out a gun. 'I won't kill you, if you shut up.'

She shot the gun. The man stood confused, he thought, he just got hit, but he looked at the wall behind him, the bullet was there.

'I can't kill you yet, just had to scare you until my guards come.'

The man looked behind him, and two guards came running and grabbed him. 'Put him back in his room' added Alicia, smirking at him.

'YOU CAN'T KILL ME' she shouted, as the guards pulled him back.

'SHUT UP YOU SLUT, I HOPE YOU DIE, NO ONE LIKES YOU, DIE, DIE,

DIE' he screamed back, trying to escape, as he flung his hands around trying to escape.

She laughed and turned around.

Nyx was still in her room, crouched down, her face buried in her legs, her fingers scratching up against her legs.

She heard a gunshot. Her mom was dead. Right?

She heard a knock on her door. Nyx clasped her hands to her mouth, it was the man, he was knocking to show her what he had done, Nyx slowly got up and tried to open the door. 'Why was your door locked from the outside?' Alicia murmured. 'What the….' Nyx said looking at Alicia. It can't be, her mom probably shot him too. She was powerful. No one could kill her.

Nyx looked away. Alicia noticed the look on her face 'Anyways I'm going out with my friends; you want me to order food?'. 'No' Alica nodded and walked away closing the door. She was sure Nyx heard the gunshot. She walked down and looked at the gunshot stain on the wall, she slid the small flower table towards it, to hide the stain.

Nyx fell on her bed and laid there for a while. She had to find out more.

She sat on her bed; her door was locked. Nyx took out the Swiss Army knife from her pocket.

The silver blade of the Swiss Army knife gleamed in the soft moonlight that filtered through the curtains, casting a mesmerizing glow over the intricate engravings on the handle. Nyx ran her fingers over the smooth surface. She took a deep breath and sliced her arm. Nyx winced in pain. She thought it would feel good, but it hurt. She examined the cut, as the blood oozed out.

'Well, I thought I would feel better...' she sighed and walked out.

The blood was dripping from her arm, and a drop fell on the white marble tiles. It glimmered in the light. A maid let out a gasp, as she saw the cut. 'Miss, do you need a?'

'No.'

# Chapter – 21

The beeping of the machines in the room seemed to drown out the sound of the TV show. Riley shifted uncomfortably in her bed, feeling the ache in her body, from being confined to the sterile hospital room, for what felt like an eternity.

As the familiar theme song of Cake Boss played on the TV, she sighed and tried to sit up. The warmth of the sun from the window hits her fragile skin. She missed being normal. But here she was, tethered to the Chemotherapy IV that delivered much-needed medication to her body. It drained all the life out of her.

She glanced down at the needle inserted into her arm, seeing the thin tube, that snaked its way back to the machine beside her bed. Each time she moved; the needle pricked her skin. She closed her eyes, trying to block out the constant beeping of the machines. The cancer had spread like wildfire, and she could not stand up for more than a minute, without feeling tired.

A nurse walked in with a tray of food. 'Food's here Riley' she said, placing a small table on her bed, the table creaked, as its legs sunk into the hard mattress.

Riley looked away, as the nurse left the room. She picked up a spoon, and scooped up some soup, the smell made her sick.

As she struggled to drink it, her door flew open and she saw Nyx standing, Riley managed a faint smile at the sight of her friend. Nyx's concern was evident, as she moved closer to the bed, her eyes scanning Riley's pale face... 'Hey, how are you?' she said walking in.

'Doing OK...I guess' Riley replied, placing the spoon on the tray. She felt a wave of nausea wash over her, as the smell of the soup lingered in the air, making her stomach churn. Trying to push through the discomfort, she picked up the spoon again, but her trembling hands betrayed her efforts.

Before she could say anything, a sudden wave of dizziness overcame Riley, and she doubled over in pain. Nyx's eyes widened in alarm, as she watched Riley's body convulse uncontrollably. Nyx got up in fear and screamed for the nurse 'HELP!' she rushed out 'HELP!'

A nurse came running in, 'CALL THE DOCTOR' she shouted to another nurse. 'What happened to her?' she asked Nyx, as she tried to move the table of her bed. 'She was fine seconds ago...I don't know, help her, she said as her voice trembled in fear.

Nyx felt a lump form in her throat. 'Is she going to be, okay?' she asked, her voice filled with worry.

'She's having a seizure; we need to stabilize her.'

The nurse rushed into the room, followed closely by the doctor. They worked quickly to stabilize Riley, but her condition deteriorated rapidly.

Riley's body continued to convulse, her breathing becoming shallow and erratic.

'Riley, please' Nyx whispered, her neck sweating, she held onto the bed and held her mouth close as she whispered. 'Please, Riley'.

'Please' her voice trembled.

As the medical team fought to save her, the room filled with a sense of desperation and helplessness. The doctor realized her heart had crashed, and he performed CPR, while Nyx stood in the corner crying, as she heard the ribs crack. But there was no response. Riley remained unresponsive, her body limp and still.

The doctor's expression hardened, as he realized the gravity of the situation. He looked up, his eyes meeting Nyx's gaze with a heavy heart.

'I'm sorry, she is in an asystole,' he said, glancing over at the monitor. Nyx saw the flat-line on the screen, as beads of sweat poured down her. No. No. This can't be, she just lost someone else. She looked at Riley's lifeless body, her face looked peaceful, her hair sliding down her ears.

Nyx stood in silence, her knees weak, as the nurses rushed out, calling the parents. Nyx sat next to Riley, holding her cold hand. She looked beautiful even after she died.

Patricia and Simon rushed in, staring at the shut-off monitors, and they saw the look on Nyx's face. It was true what the doctor said. It was true. Patricia dropped her coffee cup and ran to the bed and Simon stared at the body with open eyes. Nyx got up and walked out, wiping a tear from her face.

# Chapter – 22

**2 Months Later**

It had been exactly two months since she died. And three since he died. Nyx had lost her dad and a friend in three months. She never got over it. Never.

She sat in her room all day. The emptiness in her chest felt overwhelming at times, making it hard to breathe. Dexter came over, but she ignored him, but he never left, he did not give up on Nyx, like how, Alicia did. How could her mom have killed him? Why did Riley die? Why?

She was lying on her bed, thinking about the past few months. Her head throbbed from all the thinking, the moonlight shining through the curtains—the same questions running through her mind. She stared at the pearl white ceiling. Her mom was the reason for it all, she killed him, and she fired Simon, the stress must have gotten into Riley, and he could not pay for the Chemotherapy completely. It was that bitch's fault. Nyx hated her so much.

As Nyx's eyes gleamed, a smirk crept across her lips, a contrast to the tears, that had stained her cheeks.

R   e   v   e   n   g   e.

After all, she was Nyx Ada, daughter of the psychopath killer and drug dealer Alicia Ada.

# Chapter – 23

She lurked into her mom's room. Holding a needle. She stole it from the hospital. It had Diazepam. She had this thought about this day, for a long time, the needle was safely put in a box under Nyx's bed. "This should knock her out," she whispered. She jammed it into her mom's neck. Alicia jumped up "Nyx-" she said, as she got up holding her neck, she looked at the needle "Nyx- What- Are you- HELP!" Nyx shoved a pillow into her face "You won't remember this. Sleep you bitch"

Alicia's eyes closed as she dropped down on her pillow, the silk bed sheet wrinkling, as her head hit it.

Nyx chuckled, as she wiped the needle of any fingerprints, she slowly wrapped Alicia's fingers around it to make it look like she did it to herself, suicide. Now all she had to do was find the secret passage.

It was 3 a.m.

She walked slowly into the office, locking the door behind her.

Nyx moved with cautious steps, her eyes scanning every corner for any clue. As she carefully overturned files and books, the faint glow of the moon, through the window highlighted the determination on her face. Her fingers brushed against a cold; metallic object hidden beneath a stack of papers. Her phone rang.

"Who the fuck is!" It was Dex.

'Hello?'

'You are not replying to my texts, are you OK?' 'Yes. I'm taking care of something.

'Need help?'

'Actually...Yeah...3rd floor, first window, there's a tree near the window you can climb, come through the first gate, no security. Don't come from the back.'

'Okay, see you Nyx' 'Yeah, bye.'

Dex listened in awe, as he closed the window he had just climbed through.

"So, you stabbed her with a fucking needle?" he lifted up his finger and pointed it to his throat trying to reenact it.

"Yeah" Nyx said still looking around.

"OK, where do I start?" he asked looking at the mess she made.

"Umm, I haven't touched those books in the cabinet there, look there," she said pointing at it.

Dexter walked over, staring at the books, there were so many, but one, in particular, caught his eye.

"Hey, Nyx, usually in movies, books like this are the key to the secret passage-" he joked pulling it out, the laced book fell from his hands as a door opened up, "Fuck, yeah" Nyx whispered as she put down a stack of books.

"Damn, so it's real," he said looking into the tunnel. Nyx and Dexter exchanged excited glances.

"I knew you would help me" Nyx laughed.

They walked in slowly looking around. "What do we do?"

"Walk around, look for clues, anything helps" Nyx replied as she wiped sweat off her nose. "Find all the drugs, and the captured guy in here, and then the best part, call the police and expose her." They walked around for a while, examining the passage. They heard something. Or, someone. It sounded like footsteps. "Do you think it's your mom?", "No, she won't wake up for a while" They looked behind them.

Shit. Shit.

Someone was standing, but they could not make out who it was, they saw something in his hands.

"Run" Nyx whispered as she saw a knife shining.

She held Dexter's hand, and ran, pulling him. "Fuck, HE HAS A KNIFE?" he asked, looking at Nyx. She nodded as she pushed her hair back from her face.

They sprinted through the dark, twisting passageways, their heartbeats pounding in their ears. The footsteps behind them grew louder and closer. Nyx and Dexter reached a fork in the passage and without hesitation, Nyx pulled Dexter to the right, trusting her gut instinct. Her legs hurt, every inch, but she could not give up. They ran as fast as they could. The man behind them was running like a fucking sprinter, his knife gleaming. But he stopped. He looked at them closely as he slowly lowered his knife. There was a small light at the end. Nyx gasped. Oh god. He left them alone. But they ran, ran deep into the passages. Dexter stopped running after a while "He stopped, running, Nyx, let's sit" he said gasping for air. Nyx nodded and held her knees. She slid to the floor taking a deep breath, her jacket now sticking to her because of the sweat, she slowly leaned back and stretched out her legs.

"Well, I guess we have to stay here for a while" Dex sighed.

It had been about two hours. Dexter checked the time, 6 am. His parents must have realized, he wasn't home.

But he had to stay, well, not like he could get out of here. Nyx opened her eyes, and looked around, she got up peeking to the sides. "Let's get out of here before that guy comes back and kills us."

They walked for a while trying to get out, when they heard the same footsteps again. They looked at each other and slowly turned around.

Nyx squinted her eyes, as she tried to make out who it was. Simon.

"Simon?"

His shirt was red with blood, and his eyes were wet and red. A small knife sticking out of his pocket. He looked like a zombie, he was in a trance, his eyes not able to focus.

"Are you OK?" Nyx asked stepping closer, she heard Dexter whisper "Nyx, wait, don't go near him."

"He's high on something," Dexter said, stepping away and grabbing Nyx's shoulder. He was referring to drugs, he thought Simon was high on drugs.

"Simon?" Nyx asked again as she walked closer.

"Nyx, he is still here," Simon replied, tears streaming down his face, his eyes bulging, his voice echoed through the tunnels.

"Who is?"

# Chapter - 24

"Ryan," Simon said stepping back, pulling his gloves off "Dad?" Nyx whispered, "But my mom, she-"

"She shot him, right?" Dex completed stepping in front of Nyx, trying to make sure he wouldn't hurt her.

Simon looked away, as a drop of tear went down his cheek. His eyes looked like Riley's, but she was...

"Simon. What happened to Dad?" She blurted, trying to push away her thoughts about Riley.

"He is not dead," he replied. "What! but I saw the blood, she killed him, I know it, he died, in the warehouse, that day, I heard the gunshot" Nyx stammered looking at him.

"She shot his arm," Simon said, trying not to look into Nyx's eyes. So, he was...

She stood frozen, her eyes wide with disbelief. The dimly lit passage seemed to close in around her. But it can't be. It can't. What about the funeral, what about the...

"You're joking" she said holding her head as it throbbed in pain. 'How?' She thought he died. Where is he? What the fuck is.... "Well, if he is alive, where the fuck is he Simon" Dexter muttered.

Simon walked back and unlocked a small door, he wiped his forehead, and smeared it on his shirt, and stepped back.

A frail-looking man stepped out, he covered his head and body with a blanket that had stains on it. His face was full of scars, and he clutched his arm tightly. Ryan looked up at Nyx. "Hi Nyx" he whispered, his voice trembling in pain.

"DAD," Nyx said running over to him.

But he fell, held his hand and screamed in pain.

"Fuck, DAD, what happened-" she said falling to the floor, removing the blanket covering his arm.

It was shot. By Alicia, that day, in the warehouse, but it was not treated well. A blood-stained bandage was falling off and the skin was rotting. He tried to smile, looking at Nyx, and held his other hand out to push her tangled hair back. "I was r4455, I wanted you to find out about Alicia, I wanted you to be safe, but I did not want you to know it was me, if Alicia found out, she would hurt you, I tried escaping many times, but I was caught" he whimpered.

"Your Mother is not good, she….." he coughed up blood, and Nyx shrieked as she held him, the smell of blood hitting her again.

"Her house, the business, it's all drug money….." he said trying to sit up. Nyx cried as she held him, her shirt stained with his blood. She was not crying about Alicia, but she realized, this was her last chance to talk to him.

She thought he died. But she had a chance now. So much to tell him, about everything.

"Dad. Please, let's not-" she cried as her stomach churned in pain.

"You have to know Nyx, we have to put her behind bars, a prison for the insane-" he argued in pain. "I have the proof, of her doing this, it's all filed, under your mattress, I asked Simon to put it there, just give it to the police Nyx."

"OK" she whispered, closing her eyes, trying to soak in his voice for the last time before he would go silent forever.

"I'm sorry, you thought I died. I could not tell you. I had one phone, Simon, he sneaked in to help me, we tried to kill Alicia, but he lost his daughter, and he went psycho, he would walk around, with a knife threatening to kill anyone, he thought you were the reason Riley died, because you were the last person with her, he thought you were not good Nyx. But I told him, I don't think I can live anymore, I'm sick, my hand is infected and I'm really sick" Ryan whispered taking a deep breath, looking into his daughter's green eyes.

"Simon call 911, help him, please, Dexter call the police, get help, " she shouted wiping the blood off her dad's chin, the smell hitting her again.

"You can deal with it again Nyx, my death, you can, please do the right thing, destroy Alicia, please, Nyx, I want her to….." he gasped.

He took his last breath. And died in front of Nyx. Again, But now. It was Real.

R e v e n g e ?

# Chapter – 25

It hurt. Everything did. She went through it again. All over again, she hated Ryan for that. Who dies twice?

Well, who kills twice? Alicia.

Alicia Ada.

That little piece of shit.

The police sirens blared through the roads. The red and blue lights illuminating the roads. Nyx had called them.

Alicia was arrested.

Nyx stood looking at her, Alicia's face looked powerless. It happened so fast- The look on Alicia's face.

It was worth it all. Everything. Every fucking thing.

She got a life sentence. She was going to die in prison.

R   e   v   e   n   g   e

Nyx is confused. Dexter is. Ryan was. Riley was. Simon is. But Nyx was happy. She was. For once. After a long time.

Dexter needed a psychologist, he witnessed a, well, a death, again. It's hard you know.

It is.

Her dad was peaceful now, after his ex-wife was in prison, his dying wish. Everything happened so fast.

It was crazy. Alicia was.

Nyx was.

She was psychotic. Her mind was.

Isn't everyone's mind like that? Or is it just me?

# Epilogue

October 14th, one year after the arresting of Alicia Ada, and the deaths of Ryan Edin and Riley Simon.

Their footsteps rustled as they stepped on dry leaves, they slowly walked in silence.

The crisp autumn air hitting their faces, they stopped when they reached the secluded warehouse, that was now turned into a de-addiction retreat for drug addicts, tucked away in the woods, within the trees, Nyx quietly led Dexter to the back of the warehouse, her footsteps floating, as she tried to avoid the leaves and twigs.

The cemetery was quiet. Nyx's voice broke the stillness like a delicate whisper, barely audible, amidst the whispers of the autumn breeze.

'Lay them down there, will you' Nyx whispered stepping over the grave, as she handed Dexter a bouquet of Lilies.

'Where?' he asked softly grabbing the white bouquet 'In between the graves.'

Nyx replied, as she pressed her arms together. She watched as Dexter knelt down and placed the bouquet gently on the grass, between the resting places of Ryan

Edin and Riley Simon. The scent of the flowers mingled with the earthy smell of the soil.

'Thanks' Nyx sighed, standing straight as she blinked away tears, her knees weak. Dexter stood up placing his hand on her shoulder, they stood in silence, as the sun died below the horizon, casting long shadows over the graves, a gentle breeze began to stir, rustling the leaves of the surrounding trees of the woods. Nyx's hair danced in the wind, strands swaying softly around her face, she closed her eyes.

www.ingramcontent.com/pod-product-compliance
Lightning Source LLC
LaVergne TN
LVHW041532070526
838199LV00046B/1631